THE DARK SHADOW

THE DARK SHADOW

Mary Rhind

CANONGATE

First published in 1988
by Canongate Publishing Limited
17 Jeffrey Street,
Edinburgh, Scotland

British Library Cataloguing in Publication Data
Rhind, Mary
The dark shadow.
I. Title   II. Herriot, Alan
823'.914 [J]

ISBN 0-86241-182-3

Printed and bound in Great Britain
by Billing & Sons Limited, Worcester

For Jenny, Peter and Sarah

KINGDOM OF FIFE

St. Andrews

Crail

Cellardyke · Caves

Pittenweem

St Monans

Elie

Earlsferry

Isle of May

FIRTH OF FORTH

route of Davie and Lizzie

Gullane

Leith

Queensferry

Restalrig

Haddington

Edinburgh

BEING A MAP
SHOWING THE JOURNEY
OF DAVIE AND LIZZIE

Contents

The Visitor

The tall stranger stood on a large boulder outside the churchyard gates. Dressed from head to foot in sober black he had a grim face which somehow matched his attire. He raised a dark-sleeved arm to quieten the chattering company of villagers that had gathered before him.

'Listen, good people of the Burgh of Crail!' he cried earnestly. 'And mind you listen well!'

A large and noisy crowd jostled each other in the afternoon sunshine as they struggled to hear his words. News of the arrival of the visitor had spread like wild-fire through the little fishing village. People had rushed excitedly from all over the place towards the Marketgate where the stranger was to speak. All were now straining their ears to catch what the man was saying.

Lizzie clutched Davie's hand tightly and was thankful to have her brother beside her, pushed and shoved as they were by the people round about them. Although the man was shouting, it was hard for them to hear anything clearly from where they stood. Davie leant over to speak to her.

'Come on, Lizzie! Let's see if we can get nearer the front. I can't hear the mannie from here.'

He squeezed his way carefully through the gathering guiding his sister after him by the arm. Davie was slim and tall for his seventeen years. Lizzie, six years younger, was much shorter and found herself almost suffocating as he dragged her between the long full skirts of the womenfolk with their aprons stinking of fish guts. They had all rushed straight up from the harbour when word of the visitor had reached them.

At last Davie and Lizzie reached the front of the throng and Lizzie was thankful to breathe cooler and sweeter air again. From her new position the voice of the preacher was almost deafening but at least she could hear what he was saying.

'No man shall be saved but by the Word of God alone!' he shouted vehemently and paused significantly to let the statement sink in to the assembled company. He shook a fist vigorously. 'The Mass is a blasphemy, hear you! The praying to Saints is idolatry! To believe that their relics have any power today is superstition! The priests have made themselves rich through the weakness of you the people! And you. . .' he pointed accusingly as he glanced meaningfully from one face to the other '. . .you, my good people of Crail, who had so many clergy at *your* church living off *your* money, you should know!'

The crowd stood watching him in stony silence. They had seen many a travelling preacher in the last year and knew well not to commit themselves or otherwise to a speaker until they had heard the man out. The preacher took this as agreement and continued triumphantly,

'But no longer! Those days are past now! A new light is dawning on the land! The light of the True Word of God!'

Lizzie could sense a general shifting of position and restlessness among those behind her. It seemed as though the people were not all so convinced as the speaker had assumed but he continued nevertheless.

' Prayer, my good people! Prayer to Almighty God alone! And most importantly, obedience to the Word of the Holy Bible.

These are the only steps on the path to salvation!' He cleared his throat and continued gruffly. 'Remember also to keep the Sabbath Day holy! There must be no bartering or selling on the Sabbath, nor work of any kind, and that includes fishing!' He scanned the crowd in front of him with a knowing look.

Lizzie fidgeted, twisting her long golden hair round and round her fingers. She did not understand the Reformers but they always seemed to be shouting and that made her nervous. A murmur in the gathering grew stronger. At length a brave soul at the back called out,

'But Mister! The people of this town were given a special Royal Charter to allow us to fish on the Sabbath by no less than King Robert the Bruce himself. And it was to be for all time!'

The speaker ignored the comment.

'Last year, Mister Knox warned you of the evils of fishing on the Sabbath and yet we have heard that the fishermen of Crail still set forth on the Lord's Day. In future, woe betide anyone caught breaking God's law! And mind, it will not go unnoticed!'

Davie listening grimly to the man's address knew only too well how the Reformers would find out. Their step-father, Walter, had been converted to the new religion the previous year and was now more than willing to report those practising the old ways of the Catholic church. Fortunately, he mused, Walter was at sea just now otherwise he would certainly have been up beside the speaker having his say as well.

Davie was startled out of his thoughts to see the visitor jump down off the stone where he had been holding forth.

'Each parish is charged to look after the burden of their sins, that is, the lame, the blind, the deserving poor and the widows and fatherless.'

He went forward and took Lizzie by the hand. 'Come, lass!' he commanded in his rough voice, 'Sit ye upon the stone!'

Lizzie, bewildered and confused by this sudden attention, felt his powerful hands around her waist as he lifted her up easily to a sitting position on the stone.

11

'Look long at this little girl, my people!' he bellowed, and Lizzie cowered with fright beside him. 'She is blind, as most of you well know! But her blindness is caused by the sin of you all! Therefore you, you my good people, are charged by God to look after her. She is the burden God has placed upon you. . .She is the reminder of your sinfulness. . .The Word of God in the Holy Bible has proclaimed it. . . . . .!'

Lizzie heard no more. Without realising it she had broken away from the speaker's grasp and slid off the boulder where she had been placed. She was now running - running she knew not where, nor indeed cared, just so long as she was away from his shouting, his ranting, his accusations. She ran heedlessly, his words rolling round and round in her head. Blind! She was the burden! God's burden on the people of Crail!

Tears streamed down her face as she felt her way along the street - her arms in front to ward off any unusual obstacle, though she knew her way well about the village. Her bare feet began to hurt as she stubbed them on stones in her haste. She could hear the crowd shouting angrily behind her, not knowing whether it was herself or the preacher to which they were directing their anger.

Gradually she became aware of footsteps running behind her. 'Lizzie!' It was Davie. She turned and fell into his arms.

'Oh, Davie, Davie!' she cried, sobbing pitifully against him. 'How could he say such things about me? Why did he shout at me so? I hate him! I hate him!'

Davie held her close. What could he say to comfort her? Not to pay any heed to the preacher? It was not possible.

Times had been hard for them all at Crail since Mister Knox's sermon at the Kirk the year before and their lives had been in continuous turmoil with all the new church reforms and regulations. His own life had been particularly disrupted for he had been studying at St Leonard's College in nearby St Andrews, but this year riots and unrest between the Protestant Reformers and the supporters of the Old Faith had so upset the studies at the College that it had been impossible to hold the examinations. Davie had, therefore, spent most of the summer at home in Crail.

'Come on, Lizzie,' he said eventually. 'Let's go and sit on the cliff-top.'

They walked in silence along the cliff path, their faces towards a salty breeze coming in off the sea. Above her Lizzie could hear the screeching of gulls as they wheeled overhead before swooping down effortlessly over the sea. Below her at the bottom of the steep grassy cliff she could hear the waves of the Firth of Forth rolling into the shore and then rumbling out with a sucking noise over the shingle. Normally these sounds would have delighted her, but today the preacher's harsh words blotted out all other thoughts.

Davie found a sheltered spot for them just below the top of the cliff and they sat down together in silence for a while. Davie felt so powerless to help her. He shook his head in disbelief. It surely could not be the wrath of God that had caused his Lizzie to be blind?

She had not always been so. Davie could remember the time when he was about her age and Lizzie had been a toddler. She had been able to see then, and they were happy times. Their father, Robert Cunningham, was a fisherman who had plied the Firth of Forth in his small boat to make a living for them all, while his wife Jeannie helped with the baiting, gutting and selling.

Most of the time there were plenty of fish to be caught round the coast of Fife, but once a year in the springtime, when the fish were scarce locally, Robert Cunningham would set sail for Orkney hoping for better luck there.

It was during the Orkney trip that fateful year that the worst March storms within living memory occurred. The winds howled round their little cottage by the harbour for days on end and the spray rose through the air right over the harbour wall as the waves dashed furiously against the stones.

One night when it was dark and wild, Davie was sitting in their house with his mother. Little curly-headed Lizzie was asleep on Jeannie's lap and a cheering fire crackled in the hearth. They huddled together listening to the sound of the wind buffeting the sides of their little dwelling.

13

Suddenly, several of their fisher friends burst into the room. In their arms they carried the dripping wet and lifeless body of Robert Cunningham. His boat, they stammered, had been dashed against the skerries at the entrance to the harbour on his return from Orkney. His body and those of his crew had been found washed up on the harbour beach.

When she saw her husband's body Jeannie half-rose, scarcely grasping that the thing she had so often feared had actually come to pass. Mindless of the child on her lap she stepped forward, then swayed and fainted. Lizzie was thrown forward into the fireplace hitting her head against the hearth. Davie, whose attention had been on his mother and the body of his father, started as he heard his sister's screams. The next few moments had passed in a blur of panic and shouting that he would never forget for the rest of his life. He grabbed his sister from the flames and tore off the burning blanket which had been wrapped around her. The blanket had saved her body from any lasting injury but her face was all charred and she had a bad cut on her head.

For several days she had lain, at times screaming with pain, at other times moaning softly, too young to realise what had happened to her. It was expected that she would not survive. But, by the time her father was buried and her mother beginning to accept the loss of her husband, it was clear that little Lizzie was going to pull through. They also realised that she would never see again.

Davie smiled despite himself and chuckled as he sat now with his sister on the cliff-top, remembering how they had followed the advice of Mistress Thompson, a wise old woman of the village. She had recommended rubbing fish oil into Lizzie's face daily, and so every night for almost two years Jeannie Cunningham had faithfully done just that. It was a joke to them all now, but there was no doubt that the advice had worked. Lizzie was a beautiful child without the slightest trace of a scar on her young face.

Lizzie was surprised to hear Davie chuckling when things seemed so awful to her.

15

'What's so funny, Davie?' she asked uncertainly. 'I can't see anything to laugh about.'

'Sorry! I was just remembering all that awful fish oil we used to put on your face after the night of the accident,' said Davie.

'Oh!' said Lizzie, surprised at his train of thought. She did not remember much about that night herself but often in her sleep she dreamt a terrible dream and each time it was the same. In her dream it was always dark and she could feel herself falling rapidly down, down, down, powerless to stop herself. All around there would be shouting and screaming as through the blackness, flames and sparks flew everywhere. Then suddenly she would feel a searing pain in her head. After that everything went completely black and she could not see any sparks or flames any more. All she was aware of then were her own screams and of Davie shouting 'Lizzie! Lizzie!' Then she would be conscious of a dark, dark shadow as black as death itself bending over her as she lay on the cold ground after her fall. In vain she would struggle, trying to wrench herself from his grasp as the dark shadow lifted her. She never discovered what awful fate awaited her for at this point she always woke from the nightmare screaming, usually to find her mother bending over her telling her that it was only a dream.

Lizzie shivered in spite of the lovely day. She had got used to her blindness over the years. She was even able to help her mother gutting the fish, baiting hooks and in the evenings spinning wool for their clothes. When there were no jobs to do she would go down to the harbour and listen to the stories of the old fishermen who sat around watching the younger men unloading their exotic cargo from over the sea. Now, with the visitor's words still ringing in her ears she began to realise that no matter how able she was, her blindness was always going to set her apart from other people. Somehow it seemed that everything was tied up with the new Reformers, all of them loud and most of them angry. She just did not understand anything anymore.

'It's all that Mister Knox's fault,' she declared suddenly. 'He started all this.'

'Aye! You could be right, Lizzie.' Davie replied slowly, twisting a bit of wiry grass in his hands as he spoke. 'He fairly seems to be stirring up his followers to throw out the old ways of worship. Remember last year when he gave that sermon at the Kirk here.'

Lizzie nodded, shuddering at the memory, 'Aye, I do that. It was so scary!'

Davie had to agree. He had been frightened too by the turn of events that day. John Knox had given such a rousing sermon against idolatry and ornaments in the church that most of the people listening had started to ransack the place. They had torn down the statues and carvings, gathered all the vestments and drapes together and burnt the lot.

'It was such a pity,' said Davie as he remembered that terrible day. 'The clergy may well be far too wealthy but it seems such a waste to burn all that beauty and art. To my way of thinking the old church won't last much longer.'

'Makes no difference to me if they burn all the statues and ornaments as I never saw them anyway,' she said, 'but it's horrible the way everyone is so cross and severe now. It used to be that any Reformers who spoke out against the Church were liable to be burnt at the stake or at least thrown into prison. Now it's the other way round, the Reformers have the upper hand and they're burning Catholic priests who won't conform to their way of thinking. Anyway, that's what the old fishermen are saying and they hear all the news that's going.'

'At least there's been no burnings near here for a while,' said Davie, 'but it does seem as if human nature doesn't alter much whatever religion a man follows. And Walter's the worst.'

Their new father, Walter, was indeed one of the most ardent Reformers. Everyone knew to be careful what they said in his presence in case he reported them or, worse, decided to set them on the straight and narrow himself by visiting them with a band of ruffians.

'Aye,' agreed Lizzie. 'I wish Mother hadn't married him. I suppose she needed someone to support us after Father died, but he's so strict and he doesn't treat Mother well either, even though she never complains.'

Davie got up and kicked a stone over the cliff edge.

'Well, Lizzie, there's not a lot we can do about that. But talking of Mother, we must go now. She'll be wondering where on earth we are.'

He helped his sister gently to her feet and they set off in the direction of their harbour home. Lizzie held his hand as they went and said little. The afternoon's events had for the present been pushed to the back of her mind but they were not forgotten.

Triduana's Legacy

Jeannie Cunningham was setting a kettle over the fire when Davie and Lizzie burst into the room. They were both breathless from running down the steep hill to their little fisher cottage which nestled at the side of the harbour. She looked at their faces worriedly.

'I heard what happened from some of the fish-wives,' she said grimly. 'The visiting preacher also came down here after he'd finished to see if Walter was at home. What a dreadful man! I was glad to be able to tell him that Walter was still away at sea. Oh, Lizzie, dearie! Are you all right?'

'Aye, Mother,' replied Lizzie in a quavering voice. 'I was just awful frightened by him.' To her dismay the tears rushed to her eyes again and she broke down and wept in her Mother's arms.

'And no wonder if all I heard was true,' said Jeannie holding Lizzie close to her. 'I gave that man a piece of my mind when he called here I can tell you! He'd no business to be saying things like that, scaring a young lassie out of her wits. God knows your blindness is not an easy thing to bear but it was an accident not

19

the wrath of God that brought it about. It has nothing to do with the sins of the people of Crail or the preacher for that matter and I told him so, Walter or no Walter!'

'She'll be fine, Mother!' Davie reassured his mother swiftly as he saw the tears beginning to well up in her eyes too. 'Just a wee bit shaken.'

He knew that Jeannie blamed herself for Lizzie's blindness and he worried about them both. It would be difficult for Lizzie as she got older. Blind people often ended up as beggars because it was so difficult for them to earn a living in any other way. But Jeannie had refused to let Lizzie beg and had instead taught her to do most of the things a sighted person could do.

When Lizzie had been small Jeannie had hoped she might get her daughter into a nunnery when she was older. After all, her own brother, Andrew, was in the priory at Pittenweem and could no doubt pull a few strings for his niece. But it hadn't worked out that way.

The Reformation had come, and with the sermons of John Knox and his friends the old ways were being overturned and the monasteries shut down. Only last year a decree had been pinned to each monastery gate ordering them to open their doors to the poor and needy and those without a roof over their head. Some of the more calculating beggars had taken advantage of the situation and many of the clergy had fled. These were evil times and violent for anyone to live in, particularly if you were a woman and blind.

Now, with the cruel and unfeeling words of the visiting preacher all Jeannie's worries surfaced again.

'Oh, Lizzie, Lizzie!' she murmured desperately. 'What are we going to do with you?'

Davie was still standing in the doorway watching his mother's and sister's anguish. He took a step towards them.

'Look Mother,' he said slowly and quietly, 'I do have an idea which might help Lizzie. Come and sit down both of you and listen to me.'

'An idea to help Lizzie?' echoed Jeannie surprised by his suggestion. 'What on earth are you talking about laddie?'

Lizzie too was startled at his words. She turned towards him. 'What is it, Davie? What is it? Come on, tell us!' she cried.

'Come on over and sit down and I'll tell you both about it,' he replied smiling at their curiosity. He led Lizzie over to a raised bed of turf covered with some well-flattened heather which was beside the fire. There was a blanket thrown over the top. This served as a bed at night for the family and a seat during the day. They sat down together and Davie beckoned to his mother.

Jeannie wiped her eyes quickly on her apron and went over wonderingly to join them on the seat.

'Well Davie, what is it lad? Come on, out with it!'

'Well,' he faltered, 'it was Mister Duncanson, the head of St Leonard's College, who first put the idea into my head.

'We were walking one day earlier this year near St Triduana's Altar in St Andrews. I had been talking about Lizzie and he just happened to mention that St Triduana was well known for curing those with eye troubles. 'Do you know about her?' he had asked. I had to admit that I didn't so he told me the whole story.

'Long, long ago when our country was inhabited by the people they call the Picts, Triduana, a holy lady, came as a missionary from England. Her zeal was apparent to all but she was also beautiful and the fame of this loveliness spread throughout the land. It was not long before King Nechtan himself heard of her beauty, and he determined to have her for his wife. To this end, he sent messengers to ask her to marry him, but each time she sent them away with the answer that she was already committed to God.

'The messengers arrived with increasing frequency and finally, in exasperation, Triduana asked one of them, 'What does so great a King desire of a poor virgin dedicated to God?'

'The obedient messenger replied, 'He desires for himself the most excellent beauty of your eyes.'

Davie paused and got up to kick back a log which had fallen out of the fire.

'And what happened next, Davie?' cried Lizzie eagerly jumping up and down in her impatience to know the rest of the story. Her mother smiled but even she was keen to hear more.

21

'Well, Lizzie,' continued Davie sitting down again, 'Triduana did not answer him right away, but ordered the messenger to be made comfortable while she decided upon her answer. She realised that it could now only be a matter of time before the King came himself with an armed party to carry her off by force to his stronghold. It became clear to her therefore that the situation was getting desperate but she shrank from the course of action which she knew now was the only way of deterring the King's attentions. Eventually she went out and after choosing a sharp stick from a thornbush she gouged out her eyes and skewered them on the thorn. Then, supported by her friends and in agony of pain, she made her way back to the unfortunate messenger.'

'Ugh!' exclaimed Lizzie, shocked by the idea that any one could think of doing such a thing. 'How could she? It must have been awful sore!'

'I suppose it's all she could think of,' said Davie matter-of-factly, 'but she certainly must have been very brave. When the messenger saw her coming with her face bleeding, of course he was aghast. Triduana thrust the thorn at him,

'Your Lord and King demands the beauty of my eyes. Then willingly I give them to him!'

'She heard no more from the King on the subject of marriage and it is said, in legend, that he himself gave up his throne and after a time became a monk.

'Blind though she was, Triduana continued her mission of teaching and preaching throughout the land. When she grew too old for travelling she settled down at a place called Restalrig in Lothian where she devoted herself to prayer and healing.

'On her death, the spring beside her humble dwelling was discovered to have healing properties, particularly for the eyes, and the Well has become a place of pilgrimage. People travel the length of the country to seek healing from its celebrated waters and many believe themselves to have been cured through the intercession of the Saint.'

Davie paused and looked towards his mother.

'When Mister Duncanson had told me the whole story I determined to take Lizzie there myself one day. I asked him if he thought it really possible that complete blindness could be cured by such a Well.

'Mister Duncanson did not answer me straightaway. He remained thoughtful for a while, but then he spoke.

'Yes,' he replied, 'I, personally, do believe it's possible. I have heard of many who have found relief or cure there for their eyes. How else would it have become such a popular place of pilgrimage in this country were there not some substance to the tales. Why! People come from England to obtain benefit from the holy Well of Triduana.'

'Then I shall indeed take Lizzie there when I am finished my studies and when she is a little older,' I told him.

'At this he frowned.

'Look, Davie, perhaps I shouldn't be saying this, but if I were you I would take your sister to the Well at Restalrig as soon as possible. It's only a matter of time now before they abolish places of pilgrimage. You know how bitter the Reformers are towards anything which smacks of idolatry and superstition.'

'And do you think that pilgrimages are idolatrous or superstitious?' I asked him.

'Perhaps for many, yes,' he replied carefully, 'but I know this, that if it were my sister I would at least give it a try.'

Silence fell over the little room as Davie finished speaking. He stood up and went over to the fire again.

'Now,' he said slowly, 'it seems the time has come to test the powers of the Well. Last month the saying of Mass was pronounced illegal and who is to say that pilgrimages won't be the next thing to be banned. One thing is certain now! Lizzie cannot stay here to be held up as an example to all and I for one don't intend to stand by and watch it.'

Jeannie looked at her son and put an arm round Lizzie.

'I just don't know, Davie. You've fairly sprung this on us. Lizzie is still so young. It's a long way to go for a wee lassie especially when times are dangerous. How would you travel? Where would you stay when you got there? Have you given any thought, laddie, to what it might involve?'

'Aye, Mother, that I have! I've thought about it a fair bit this last month or two while I've been away from college,' said Davie eagerly, looking excitedly at her, pleased to be able to tell someone of his plans at last. 'First I thought we'd walk along the coast to Pittenweem and contact your brother Andrew. There are many boats going out from Pittenweem to the Lothian shore and I'm sure he'd help us to find one.'

'Aye, I suppose he would,' replied Jeannie. Her brother was in charge of the priory at Pittenweem now that the Abbot, fearing the wrath of the Reformers, had fled. 'He should indeed be able to find a boat to take you easily enough.'

Lizzie had been sitting quietly listening to them talk, scarcely able to take in what it all meant. The chance that she might be able to see again, like everybody else, seemed too unbelievable to grasp.

'Is it really true, Davie? Might I really see again; see the blue of the sea you are always telling me about and the foam on the crest of the waves, dancing like sea horses through the water? Can it really be possible?'

'I wouldn't even talk of taking you Lizzie if I didn't think there was every chance,' said Davie, coming over to squeeze her hand. 'They say that the waters of St Triduana's Well are powerful and', he added, 'the Bible says that with God all things are possible. Even the Reformers must agree on that.'

'Och! away!' scolded Jeannie going to the fireplace where she had resurrected the fire and now had a steaming pot of limpet broth. 'Don't get the poor lass all excited! Not everyone who goes to Restalrig is cured, you may be sure. One has to accept that God may sometimes have other plans. And yet, it could be worth trying, if the waters of that Well are as renowned as Davie says for their healing powers.'

Lizzie began to chatter excitedly, asking Davie all sorts of questions about his plans and St Triduana's Well.

24

Oblivious to their lively voices, Jeannie stirred the broth and pondered over the journey her children would have to make. Times were troubled and there were many brigands on the roads. She knew homeless wanderers would not be slow to attack two young people if they thought there was money or food to be had. And yet, she thought, Davie was a grown lad now. If they could reach Pittenweem there was every chance they would find a passage across the Firth.

At length the room fell silent and all that could be heard was the crackle of flames in the fire beneath the pot. Jeannie took a taper and lit the little rush lamp in its alcove on the wall. Then she handed them each a bowl of the warming soup and settled herself on a low stool at the other side of the fireplace. They sat and talked over the whole idea as they supped.

'It's a good job Walter is away at sea,' said Jeannie suddenly as the thought struck her. 'He would never allow you to go. He hates anyone to even speak of the old ways of religion, never mind practise them. You'll have to go before he gets back, but that could be a day or two yet.'

Davie knew she was right. He could just picture his step-father's face when he learnt they had set off on such a journey. A tall, lean fisherman with a wiry strength and a rugged weather-burnt face from the constant salty spray and wind he was not an individual to be reckoned with when roused. Walter could be an angry man. Not only that but he was a well known Reformer with deep convictions and had Reformer contacts all over the place. He could soon have them stopped if he found out what they were up to. Furthermore Davie and Walter were already at loggerheads because Davie had chosen to go to college in St Andrews instead of joining his step-father on the boat as had been assumed and as indeed all the other lads of his age had done.

When they lay down that night to sleep, Lizzie smiled contentedly to herself. The episode of the shouting preacher had been completely wiped from her thoughts. A hope had been raised in her mind beyond her wildest dreams and who knew what the outcome might be?

The Journey Begins

Lizzie awoke the next morning with Davie shaking her excitedly.

'Wake up Lizzie! Come on, quickly! Get up!'

There was such an urgency in his voice that she sat up at once.

'What is it Davie? What's going on?'

'It's Walter! I can see his boat approaching the harbour. He's still a good way out and he'll have to wait for the tide to come in before he can enter it. If we want to go on this pilgrimage to St Triduana's Well we'll have to go now. Mother agrees. We may not get a chance like this again!'

Jeannie came bustling in, fussing. Lizzie could sense the anxiety in her voice.

'Come away Lizzie, you'll have to get ready now. Walter's going to be in on this tide. Here's a shawl for you for the cold and your shoes in case your feet should be sore with walking.'

She folded the shoes into the shawl and pressed the lot into Lizzie's arms.

Lizzie caressed the bundle lovingly. These were her precious shoes, which she was normally only allowed to wear on Sundays or market days. Now she could wear them whenever she wished. Made with tough hide and tied with leather thongs they always felt so smooth and soft to her hardened feet. She jumped up and down excitedly in anticipation.

Davie was given a pair of shoes too and a blanket, big enough for them both to sleep under.

'But Mother, these are Walter's!' Davie cried in dismay when she handed over the shoes. 'He'll be so cross when he finds out that you have given them to me.'

'He's not going to find out!' said Jeannie calmly and determinedly. 'I'll sell some of my wool at the next market and buy him another pair. He'll not notice before then as he has some better ones that he normally wears on Sundays.'

Davie hesitated. He knew how terrible Walter could be in a rage. 'Oh Mother, are you sure?'

'I've managed things up till now and the Good Lord willing, I shall continue to do so.' Jeannie's face relaxed into a smile touched by his anxious concern. 'Don't you worry about it, laddie. It's time you were away now. Here's a basket for you. In it are some bannocks which should keep you going for a few days and there's a wee pouch of oatmeal to use when they're done and. . . wait a minute . . .' She strode hurriedly over to the fireplace and reaching up into the chimney lum she produced a dried smoked fish. 'Here you are!' she said over-brightly to hide her emotions at their going as she placed the fish in the basket beside the rest. 'This'll put strength into your legs. Keep it in case you become tired or disheartened. It'll revive your spirits and remind you of home.' Her voice began to waver, 'Now go my children and God be with you. You'll be in my thoughts and prayers every moment you're away. I'll try my best not to tell your step-father where you've gone till dusk. I'll let him think you're away along the shore or something. He cannot stop you Davie, but Lizzie he can and will!'

Lizzie hugged her Mother tearfully. 'Goodbye, Mother. Goodbye!' she sobbed, but they were tears of excitement which she wept more than of sorrow.

They tucked their bundles under their arms and headed towards the doorway.

'Don't come out, Mother,' said Davie, 'in case the neighbours notice that we are going and mention it to Walter when he returns.' He gave a last weak smile to his mother then turned and guided Lizzie out.

Jeannie spent a while standing gazing into the fire, fighting back the tears which threatened to overwhelm her. The two most dear people in her life had just left it and she knew they had a difficult and dangerous journey ahead of them. The worst danger of all though would be from Walter, who would certainly go after them if he thought there was any chance of catching them. Fanatical himself about abolishing the old ways of religious practice he would be livid to learn that his own family, step-children though they were, had gone openly on pilgrimage. Worse, since he was the chief person in the district who reported those who did not conform to the new ways of worship to the Reformers, how would he ever be able to show face in the village of Crail were he not seen to mete out a suitable punishment to the pair for their actions. Lizzie would probably be young enough to escape blame but she shuddered to think what he would do to Davie. He would show no mercy.

Jeannie was desolate. In the heat of Davie's excitement last night it had seemed a good plan. Now she wished earnestly that she had never let them go.

She set herself to lighting a fire and fetched another fish from the chimney for Walter. Perhaps on a full stomach he might be less angry when he found out, she thought hopefully. But she knew that it was a vain hope.

Davie and Lizzie climbed hurriedly up the harbour brae. They did not take the road for Pittenweem. Instead they set off eagerly along the shoreline where there were nearly always some honest fisherfolk collecting winkles within earshot. They walked along hand in hand, feeling the springy turf beneath their feet as they went.

'We never thought yesterday that we should be doing this today,' said Lizzie gaily. She skipped along, her long golden hair flying out behind her, as she swung her precious shoes inside the shawl.

'No,' agreed Davie, remembering the awful preacher's words of the day before. 'Although I've been planning this all summer I didn't think we'd have to move so quickly.'

He turned around to take a last look at the harbour of Crail. He could see Jeannie standing outside her little red tiled house watching them and he raised a hand in farewell. A little way out from the harbour was a cluster of boats heading for home and among them he managed to pick out Walter Fisher's.

'Still too far away for him to recognise us,' he muttered to himself contentedly, but he automatically quickened his pace and Lizzie was now at a half-run to keep up with him. She laughed and sang as they went. Sad though she was to leave her mother she felt safe and secure with Davie and excited to be on such an adventure.

The sun was well up now and shining in a wide golden ribbon across the sea. Lizzie could hear the sea distantly as it broke on the furthest rocks and the gulls wailing as they made their way towards the line of incoming boats. From time to time she thrilled to the squealing of oyster-catchers and once, caught the slow swish-swish of a heron's wings as it flew leisurely past them from one rock to another. Davie described the things he saw as they walked so that she should not find the going dull. But the sounds were enough for her. She felt a bubble of joy rise up inside her as she realised that soon she might be able to look at all these things for herself.

Once or twice Davie saw someone that he recognised collecting shellfish out on the rocks and he raised a hand in greeting, but they did not stop to chat.

They kept close to the shore. To the landward side the ground rose steeply, sometimes grassy, sometimes in rocky cliffs.

29

Every so often they came to a bog where a burn trickled down from the higher ground and meandered across their way to the sea. Lizzie loved the cool oozy feeling as the mud squelched through her toes.

The late summer sun was high in the sky when they came to a bigger stream in full spate. It roared down through a gully splashing and foaming like some white wild beast. Their path should have led to a place where large boulders had been placed as stepping stones across the water but today they were half hidden by the swirling foam.

'It's no use Lizzie,' said Davie when he saw the situation. 'We can't use the stones. The water is splashing right over them. They'll be far too slippery. I'll have to wade and take you over on my back.'

Lizzie was glad. She could hear the water as it thundered before them and it was a frightening sound. Davie threw their two bundles across first and let Lizzie climb up on his back. Then with their food basket balanced precariously on one arm he climbed gingerly down the bank into the rushing river. The water was even deeper than it had looked and Lizzie clung tightly to her brother as he felt around tentatively with his feet to secure a firm footing on the slippery bottom. Twice he almost slipped and Lizzie screamed as she felt him go but her voice was scarcely audible above the splash and rumble of the torrent. She tightened her grip around his neck and was glad of his broad shoulders which prevented her slipping sideways.

Suddenly while they were still struggling in the river a deep, booming man's voice shouted above the roar of the water.

'Don't move an inch or I shall drown you both. Hand over your money!'

Lizzie clutched Davie desperately and froze as she felt Davie stiffen. Davie balancing delicately in mid-stream glanced around quickly trying to place the direction of the voice but the noise of the water made it impossible to locate. Suddenly a swarthy figure leapt out from behind a whin bush.

31

'We have no money!' cried Davie earnestly. 'We're only two poor travellers!'

Then he recognised the grinning face.

'Alan Maynard!' he smiled relaxing. 'Of all the rotten tricks! Just wait till I get out of this water!'

The stranger laughed. 'Aye, Davie! It's been a long time since we've seen each other. Will you forgive me for scaring you if I offer you a bite to eat?'

Davie pulled a face at him as much as to say he would think about it and set his concentration back to getting safely across with Lizzie without falling in. When they finally reached the bank without mishap Alan took Lizzie off his back and lowered her to the ground. Lizzie could smell a mixture of wood and seaweed smoke on his clothes and could guess that he had until very recently been lighting a fire. As he lifted her down Lizzie noticed that his arms were stronger than Davie's though he was about the same height. His coat was of a coarse and woollen cloth common in those parts but his shirt was smooth and silky. She had felt material like it once before at the harbour at Crail when the men were unloading and knew that such stuff came from far across the seas. It was material that only rich men could afford and Alan did not seem to be that so she wondered how he could have come by it.

'And is this little Lizzie?' he asked with the same deep sonorous voice that had shouted from behind the whin bush. He set her down. 'My, how you've grown!'

She smiled politely. She was not sure who he was but he seemed friendly enough now and his arms, strong as they were, had been gentle.

'You scoundrel, Alan!' said Davie clapping him good-naturedly over the shoulders. 'Well, well! It's certainly a while since we set eyes on each other.' He glanced quickly at him and like Lizzie he too noticed the silk shirt. 'You look well, man! And prosperous if I may say so! What are you up to these days, apart from frightening the life out of innocent travellers, that is?'

Alan laughed partly at the success of his little joke and partly because he was pleased to see old friends again. 'Come on up to the cave that I live in,' he said, 'and I'll tell you all. Come on, Lizzie. You can come with me.'

Lizzie felt herself being lifted up into his strong arms again and he strode off leaving Davie to pick up their bundles and follow.

Pirate Meeting

Alan led them up a grassy slope then down again into a hollow near the shore where there stood a row of enormous caves hollowed out of the pink sandstone. Davie and Lizzie had been here a few times. It was said that St Adrian and his band of followers had hidden in these caves when the Vikings in their longships had attacked their monastery on the Isle of May out in the Firth. Here the monks were able to look out over the sea towards their former home and in one of the caves they had left traces of their occupation, several crosses carved into the stone wall. Davie had in the past lifted Lizzie up to let her feel them and it was into this cave now that Alan Maynard disappeared with Lizzie, where there was, as she had so rightly guessed, a smouldering fire of dried seaweed and driftwood.

'There you are Lizzie,' said Alan brightly as he placed her carefully down on a flat stone beside the fire, 'you sit there. I expect you're ready for a seat after all that walking.'

'Aye,' replied Lizzie shyly. 'I am that! It's nice and warm in here, isn't it!' She stretched out her hands towards the warmth of the fire. Davie coming into the cave behind them pushed in beside her.

'Come on, Lizzie! Give us a bit of room. I'm soaking after crossing that river.' He sat down on the stone beside her and Lizzie moved along it away from him when she felt how cold and wet his legs were.

Alan sat down across the fire from them and Davie watched him as he carefully tried to poke some life into the fire. He had grown since Davie had seen him last. As young boys the two of them had played together. Alan's father, Hans Maynard, was a Flemish merchant who had married a Crail woman and settled there in a house at the harbour. Back and forth he used to ply with his wares across the North Sea, until one day he was attacked by pirates and lost his life trying to defend his ship. Shortly after Alan's mother had also died, some say of a broken heart, and the boy was forced to leave Crail and fend for himself as best he might. Despite his Scottish mother he was still a foreigner in the eyes of the local people and as such unwelcome. He had been a slightly built boy of about twelve when Davie had last seen him. Now he was grown into a strapping young man, tanned by the wind and weather. His hair was a russet colour, thick and curly, not far off the colour of his weather-beaten face. Round his eyes were many lines which indicated much laughter but there was a deep scar on one cheek and another across his forehead which suggested that his life had not been all easy.

The fire suddenly sprang into flames and Alan threw on a couple of logs.

'You're looking well, Alan!' said Davie truthfully, delighted to see his former playmate again now that he had recovered from the shock of their meeting. 'How're things with you?'

Alan grinned. 'You see it all,' he replied gesturing broadly round the cave. 'This is home for the time being.'

'Well, I think this is a lovely place,' said Lizzie. It was warm and cosy beside the fire and they were so sheltered in the cave that the sound of the sea was merely a whisper in the far distance even though the tide was by this time well up. She might almost have been back in their house at Crail it felt so comfortable.

'Ah, well,' continued Alan, 'I don't stay here very often. Most of the time I work on board the ship of Alexander Lumsden.'

'What! Alexander Lumsden the pirate?' exclaimed Davie, his eyes widening with surprise. Captain Lumsden was notorious along their coast for his cut-throat attacks on shipping. 'I'm surprised you do such a thing, Alan, after what happened to your father.'

Alan shrugged. 'Aye, I suppose so, but one has to live. Besides, Captain Lumsden only attacks English ships, so it seems quite a worthy cause.' He fingered the collar of his silk shirt. 'Besides, he's good to me too. After a good haul we come ashore for a while. He has a house along the coast where I'm welcome to stay but I'm used to my own company now so I usually come here.' He shrugged. 'Come on, let's have a bite to eat and then you can tell me what brings yourself and the lovely Lizzie this way.'

Lizzie blushed at the compliment. He was treating her like a lady! She put her hands instinctively to her cheeks as she felt the blood rush to her face. Alan noticed and winked across at Davie then he got up and went to the back of the cave and produced a whole pile of bannocks and some soft white cheese wrapped in a cloth. He spread one for Lizzie then handed Davie the knife and settled down again on his stone.

'Now then,' he said, 'tell me all your news! What brings you travelling by here? It can't be for the good of your health for I watched you for a while coming along the path there and Davie was aye looking behind him as if he might be expecting to be followed. Is there someone after you? Have you done something wrong? Is your mother all right and for that matter your step-father?'

'Wheesht, man!' cried Davie laughing. 'One question at a time! Mother's fine and at home and I should think that Walter will very nearly be at home too by now for we saw his boat coming in as we left. What's more, Alan, you'll be surprised to know that in a way we are here for the good of our health, at least Lizzie is.' Then Davie proceeded to tell Alan everything about his plan. How they were headed for Pittenweem in the hopes of finding a boat to take them over the Firth of Forth to as near Restalrig as possible.

When he had finished Alan did not laugh at the idea as Davie had supposed he would. Instead he looked at them astutely and said slowly,

'And I suppose the return of your step-father had some bearing on the matter?'

'Indeed,' replied Davie gravely, 'and we have to carry on as quickly as possible in case he comes after us to try and take us back.' He glanced around nervously as he spoke as if he half expected Walter to materialise out of the shadows. 'He is so bitter towards those who practise any of the ways of the Old Faith. With us he'll be furious!'

'Well,' said Alan, 'who can blame him? After all many of the priests and clergy are rich, collecting rents and tithes often without doing a stroke of work. That's bound to make an honest, hard-working man like Walter see red.'

'How d'you mean?' said Lizzie. 'Don't the priests work?'

Davie kicked at a stone with his foot. 'That's just it, Lizzie, many of them didn't. Look at Crail, a college kirk with its provost, ten priests and all those chapels. Yet John Knox was able to just walk in and preach. There was no-one to stop him as the clergy were all absent. That church for its size should have been going like a fair on a Sunday.'

Lizzie still didn't understand. 'But wasn't Mister Knox a priest too?'

Alan laughed and slapped his knee. 'Ha!' he exclaimed. 'I do believe you would have made a scholar too, just like your brother, if you hadn't been a woman!'

Davie made a face at him. He was used to teasing from the lads at Crail about the fact that he was at college.

'You're right Lizzie,' he continued, ignoring Alan's little dig at him. 'John Knox was a priest, but of the new kind who have now broken away from the mainstream of the church. They don't believe in the clergy having too much wealth but mind you they still do well enough for themselves. They also believe that the services should be held in the ordinary tongue of the people.'

'Aye, aye!' said Alan heartily, 'I certainly agree with that!'

'You surprise me, Alan!' replied Davie with a twinkle in his eye. 'I'd have thought that you of all people who are half Flemish would see the point in having one language that can be used throughout Europe.'

'You're pulling my leg now, Davie,' retorted Alan. 'Anyway, since I never go near a church the point doesn't matter. What do you say Lizzie? Come on, help me to argue with your brother!'

Lizzie laughed. 'I say,' she said slowly as if deliberating some deep point, 'that I'm still hungry. Is there another bannock?' She giggled at her own joke.

Alan laughed too. 'Of course! Come on eat up! There's plenty of it! Let's you and I leave Davie to his own arguments!'

'Och! I don't suppose anyone would get to the bottom of it all no matter how long they argued for,' said Davie standing up. 'We'll have to go anyway, Alan. We want to reach Pittenweem before dark. And there's still Walter to worry about!' As he remembered Walter again he ran outside and quickly looked back along the way they had come but there was no sign of anyone approaching. He went back into the cave. Lizzie still had most of a bannock to eat.

'Come away Lizzie. We've got to get going. Bring the rest of that with you.'

'Wait a minute,' exclaimed Alan suddenly. 'I've just had an idea! Why don't I come with you and take you to see Alexander Lumsden, my Captain? It's just possible that he might actually be able to take you across the Firth himself, if he's planning to set to sea again soon.'

Lizzie was surprised. 'On a real pirate ship?' she exclaimed bouncing up and down excitedly.

Davie was more wary. He was not too sure that it was such a good idea. Pirates were not very trustworthy and Captain Lumsden had a gruesome reputation.

38

'And where will we find your pirate captain?' he asked unen-thusiastically.

'His house is in Cellardyke, not far from here,' said Alan eager to help his friends if he could. 'Hold on a minute!' He went to the back of the cave and gathered his things together into a small pack which he slung over his back.

With a quick backward glance, they set off along the coast towards the next fishing village, where Alan's pirate captain lived. They travelled as fast as they could without forcing the pace for Lizzie whose legs were shorter. She danced along happily hanging on to Davie's hand while Alan brought up the rear. It wasn't long at all before they reached the little cluster of fisher houses round the small harbour.

'It's just along here,' said Alan as he led them a little beyond the harbour and stopped at a row of larger houses. He knocked at a wooden door and it was opened by a plump, pleasant looking woman who recognised Alan immediately and smiled in greeting.

'Why! It's Alan!' she exclaimed. 'Come in, come in! The Captain's in here.'

They entered the house and the woman led them to a room on the right where there was a large bearded man sprawled in front of a roaring fire. The heat in the room was almost overwhelming but the man dressed in a heavy outer coat did not seem to notice. His face above the thick black beard was fat and round and bright red, the colour due probably to a combination of weathering and strong drink as well as the heat in the room, Davie thought. Glancing quickly round the room, Davie noticed a particularly large and beautiful cupboard. There were few indeed who could afford such a luxury. It was plain that this pirate Captain was a very wealthy man. There were also some chairs and a table. Davie was certain that he had never in his life seen so much furniture in one house let alone in one room.

He noticed all this in an instant while Alan addressed the large finely dressed gentleman at the fire.

'Good morning, sir!'

'Good morning to yourself, Alan,' replied the Captain congenially. 'And what brings you here today? We did not expect to see you back again so soon, but you are welcome nevertheless. Come, sit you down. Are these friends of yours?' He waved a hand towards Davie and Lizzie.

Lizzie was a little bit disturbed by the loudness of his voice. It was deafening in the little room but would no doubt have been necessary at that strength on the deck of a heaving ship.

Alan drew up a chair for Davie and Lizzie then sat down himself beside them. He smiled at the ruddy face of the Captain reflecting the glow of the fire and introduced his two companions. Then he went on to explain that they were looking for a passage to the other side of the Forth and that he, Alan, had suggested that they come and see if the Captain could take them.

'I see,' said Captain Lumsden. He looked thoughtfully at Davie and Lizzie and nodded slowly but there was a reserved frown on his face. Alan, who knew him well, guessed that he was not keen on the idea. He said neither yea nor nay to them but muttered something to himself under his breath. They were interrupted by the woman who Davie supposed must be the Captain's wife as she brought in some steaming broth for them all. For a while they chatted about various other things as if Davie and Lizzie's journey had never been mentioned and there was a rough congenial banter between Captain Lumsden and Alan that was pleasant to listen to. Lizzie began to feel quite sleepy in the heat of the room.

At length, when they had finished eating, the pirate wiped his black bushy beard with the back of his hand and stretched out his legs as he leant back in his chair.

'It'll no' do, Alan. You are one of my best men but I cannot take your friends aboard my ship. The laddie is all right but the lassie would bring bad luck to us all. Double bad luck because she is both a lass and blind. Anything I can do on land for them I will because they are friends of yours but sail with the lassie aboard my ship, never!'

The Captain's face seemed now to become almost grotesque in the light of the flickering flames as he spoke. Alan's face fell and Davie's too. Lizzie showed no emotion at all but she was beginning to think that perhaps she did bring everyone bad luck. Was she indeed cursed as the preacher at Crail had implied? She felt like running away again as she had done the day before only here she was lost. She wasn't even sure of the doorway out.

An uneasy silence fell over the room. It was Davie who, sensing her panic, spoke up first.

'Thank you for your straight answer, Captain Lumsden. Being fisherfolk ourselves we respect your beliefs. We had planned originally to go to Pittenweem to find a boat. So we shall continue on our way and hopefully shall have better luck there.'

His speech cleared the awkward atmosphere that had arisen but he got to his feet feeling a bit unwelcome now in the pirate household. Like Lizzie, all he wanted to do now was to get out.

'We thank you and your good lady for your hospitality,' he continued stiffly. 'We'll go now. Good day Captain!'

The pirate grunted and lifted his hand in salute as Davie took Lizzie's arm and made for the door. It would be a relief to get out of the heat of the room and he supposed Captain Lumsden would be pleased to return to peace and quiet. Alan took his leave of the Captain too and followed in their wake. Once outside, he apologised for raising their hopes but Davie brushed his apologies aside.

'Don't be silly, Alan! You did your best! There's nothing lost. We'll carry on to Pittenweem and find our uncle. Thanks for all the food, you old rogue!'

'It's a pleasure to have someone to share it with,' replied Alan, and Lizzie noticed the depth of sincerity in his voice. It must be lonely indeed to live his kind of life, she thought to herself.

'Perhaps we'll meet you on the way back!' she said hopefully.

'Aye! Who knows, Lizzie?' replied Alan thoughtfully, giving her a little squeeze on her shoulders. 'Good luck lass!' He raised a hand in farewell to Davie and then turned and left them to go their separate way.

41

The Priory

Lizzie was silent and dejected as they walked away from the pirate Captain's house. Davie, holding on to her hand, sensed this.

'Don't worry, Lizzie. We'll find a boat, just you wait and see!'

They decided to leave the shore path and take to the road which lay inland a bit. Here it was quite open and safe from unexpected attack. In fact today the road was almost deserted save for a pedlar with a pack on his back in the distance ahead of them.

Davie remembered the last time he had come this road. That had been on the day of the Pittenweem Fair in July when the road had been thronged with carefree and excited people, all wending their way into the village for fun and merriment. Lizzie had not been with him that day as Mother had feared she might get lost in the crowd. The contrasting quietness of the road today was in a way quite a worry to him. If Walter should follow and come upon them now he would spot them at once. There was nowhere they could hide.

He quickened his pace instinctively even though he could see that Lizzie was tiring. It would not be long before they reached the Priory for it was only a couple of miles from Cellardyke.

'Not far to go now, Lizzie!' he said encouragingly as they descended to the Dreel Burn. There was a ford where they could wade across without getting too wet and then a gentle hill in front of them which they would have to climb.

'From the top of this hill', Davie panted to Lizzie when they were about half-way up, 'we should be able to see the Priory.'

He was right. After their climb the road levelled out and Davie could see it meandering away into the distance towards Pittenweem. The roof of the Priory was easily visible as it was the tallest building in sight.

'Can you see it?' asked Lizzie excitedly.

'Aye, Lizzie,' said Davie. 'I can that. The Priory is just ahead of us. We shall soon be there!'

'Oh good! I hope our uncle will be there.'

'Of course he will, daftie!' replied Davie. But the very same thought had occurred to him too. The Abbot had already fled because of fear of the Reformers. Who knew what might have happened to Father Andrew since they had last heard of him?

The shadows were beginning to lengthen as they approached the Priory. Beneath their feet the paths felt mossy and cool and Lizzie could hear the the wind shaking the drying autumn leaves on the trees around them.

They were dismayed to find the thick wooden Priory gates firmly shut and the place had a general air of neglect and desertion about it. Looking round Davie saw a frayed rope bell-pull and he gave a sharp pull on it. Far away within the building Lizzie heard a bell echoing. In a while there was a rattling of keys and the door of the Gate House was pulled open by a tall, rather ugly looking friar in a dark but faded robe.

'Och! It's just children,' he said to himself as much as to anyone when he saw them and in a gruff tone of voice which made it clear that he wished he hadn't bothered to open the door to them at all. 'Well, what do you want?'

'We've come to see Father Andrew,' replied Davie awkwardly. The monk had a slight squint and he was not sure which eye to look at.

43

'Oh you have have you?' he mocked. 'Well I'm afraid Father Andrew is too busy to see anyone just now. Be off with you!'

'He's got to see us!' cried Lizzie in dismay. 'He's our uncle and we've walked miles and miles to see him and we need a boat and. . .'

'Did you say your uncle?' interrupted the squinting monk, suddenly becoming flustered and wringing his hands apologetically. 'Oh dear, oh dear! You must be his sister's bairns from Crail. Come along in and I'll see what I can do for you.'

He showed them into a hallway and told them sharply to wait. Meanwhile, he went out of the building by another door and through a slit in the wall Davie could see him rapidly crossing the courtyard to the main Priory building. Left on their own, Lizzie noticed at once the cool musty dampness of the Gate House while Davie gaped in wonder at the marvellous carvings and the cupboards and settles that filled the room in which they stood.

In a few minutes they heard footsteps approaching and the familiar voice of their uncle.

'Thank you, Brother John. Thank you! Yes you did the right thing in letting them in. I'll see them of course!' And then in a rustle of robes and a jingle of keys he was there beside them. He seemed genuinely delighted to see them.

'Hello, my little Lizzie and hello, Davie! How nice and how unexpected to see you both.'

Father Andrew was a tall imposing man with a bald head. His deep penetrating eyes were set in a kindly face. He too wore a faded shabby habit. He went straight towards Lizzie and embraced her.

'Lizzie, my dear, how are you? And how is your mother? Is all well at home? What brings you travelling the roads in such troubled times?'

Lizzie laughed, unsure which question to answer first. 'Mother's fine and we've lots to tell you, Uncle, but it's quite a long story.' She wasn't sure where to begin.

'A long story, eh?' said Uncle Andrew seriously. 'Well, in that case you had better come over to the Refectory and we shall

44

see if Brother John can rustle up some tea for you. You must be hungry after your journey.'

He had a quick word with Brother John then led the two tired travellers across to the far side of the courtyard.

The Priory building was tall with several storeys. Father Andrew guided them in through a small door and up a damp stairway to a large, airy room. In the middle of the room was an enormous table surrounded by huge carved chairs and at one side a bright fire which was welcome now as the chilly evening air set in. Davie spoke hesitantly.

'I hope we are not interrupting anything important, Uncle,' he said. 'Brother John said that you were busy.'

Father Andrew threw back his head and chuckled loudly, his eyes twinkling with glee.

'Oh! That!' he laughed. 'Don't mind Brother John. That's his standard line for anyone that comes to the door that he doesn't know. Since the decree was put out last year, all monasteries have been obliged to throw open their doors to the poor and homeless. We've had some pretty peculiar customers, I can tell you, and so John tends to put off as many callers as possible. He also has to check that there aren't any lurking Reformers about, ready to rush in and tear our Priory apart and us with it.'

Lizzie was alarmed. 'Oh no, Uncle! Would they really do that?' she gasped in horror.

'No, Lizzie,' Father Andrew replied, 'I doubt it. Most of the monks who objected to the Reformers and the Reforms have already left. There are only a few of us left here now and we try not to take advantage of our position as clergy. We do our best to help the poor as we can, so I think they'll leave us in peace in the meantime. Of course it won't last for ever.' He shook his head solemnly and then to change the subject he added, 'I wonder where Brother John has got to? Wait here a moment and I'll go and see.'

He swept out of the room and Lizzie said to her brother,

'I'm glad we found Uncle Andrew. It feels safe here somehow.'

'Aye,' agreed Davie. 'It does. But Lizzie you should see the furniture and the carvings in this room. I've never seen the like of it.' And he gasped as he craned his head back to admire the intricate craftsmanship on the ceiling.

'I can already feel a soft rug on the floor,' she replied, wriggling her toes on it as if to reassure herself that it was real.

'Yes, but come over here, Lizzie,' persisted Davie and led her over to the windows where there were some ornate shutters. He placed Lizzie's hands so that she could feel the carvings. 'Feel that!'

'Aye I can,' she said. 'It's a face, isn't it? I wonder whose.'

'It tells you here,' replied Davie. 'This one is of King James the Fifth and this one his lady, Queen Mary of Guise, the Queen Regent who has just died. And this one . . .'

At this point Father Andrew returned. When he saw them he said,

'Ah! Admiring the shutters are you? Very useful indeed on cold winter nights!' He pointed to where one shutter was missing. 'Unfortunately we had to put the one for this window down to the cellar. It was a carving of Cardinal Beaton who the Reformers butchered to death at St Andrews. We thought that if they came in and saw a likeness of their arch-enemy on a shutter they would probably set fire to it immediately and bring the whole house down with it. So we decided to hide it.'

They were still admiring the shutters when Brother John came into the room staggering under a large tray laden with steaming dishes, and looking a lot more jovial than he had done at the door.

'What's this, Uncle?' asked Lizzie sniffing the air as a strange smell rose from the platters. 'I haven't had this before.' She frowned trying to guess what it might be, but it was nothing that she recognised.

'I don't expect you have,' laughed Father Andrew with his deep chuckle again. 'It's venison! There are some things that the Reformers are right about. We do very well for food. But tuck in and don't ask me where it came from! It's there for sharing.'

46

Lizzie had never tasted anything quite like it in all her life, but it was delicious and there were large slices of bread to mop up the juices. In addition Father Andrew poured Davie a cup of wine in a pewter goblet. When he felt that they had eaten their fill he poured himself a cup of wine and sat back in his chair.

'Now then, tell me the whole story,' he said.

Davie told him everything. How he had decided to take Lizzie to St Triduana's Well at Restalrig to pray for the restoration of her sight as so many others had done before them. How they had rushed away from Crail and their mother so that their step-father would not be able to follow and stop them. How they had met Alan Maynard and how he had led them to Captain Lumsden at Cellardyke. And how the Captain had refused to take them.

'And now we're here', he concluded obviously, 'hoping that you'll be able to help us find a passage to the other side of the Forth.'

'Please, please, Uncle!' pleaded Lizzie.

'Hmm,' said Father Andrew slowly. Then he looked long and hard at Lizzie before addressing Davie again.

'I admire you, Davie, my lad. I know a lot of people have gone on pilgrimage to St Triduana's Well, but at this time, with so many troubles in the Church and the country as a whole, it's either foolhardy or brave. The only thing you are right about is that if it's to be done at all it has to be done now. I'm afraid that the days of places like Restalrig and even the Priory here are numbered. The Reformers have the upper hand now.' He shook his head. 'But anyway, what are we going to do with you? We do have a little boat here at the Priory but it's on the small side. It wouldn't be safe to take it all the way across the Firth. We'll have to take you along the coast to Earlsferry where you should pick up a boat going across to Gullane on the far side. That's the route travellers take to and from St Andrews which would land you not too far from Restalrig.'

Father Andrew paused suddenly at the sound of shouting outside. Then they heard the Gate House bell echoing over the

Priory courtyard as someone pulled the rope wildly. There was a loud hammering on the Priory gates.

'Open up, you good for nothing Papists,' a man's voice shouted. 'Open up or I'll break this door down.'

Terror seized Lizzie's face. 'It's Walter!' she cried. 'He's caught up with us! He's come to take us home again. Oh no! What a beating I shall get!'

Davie looked equally perturbed. 'What will we do, Uncle Andrew? Can we leave by a back door?'

'Rubbish! You're not leaving,' stated Father Andrew in a calm matter-of-fact voice, 'not at this time of night anyway. Come quickly with me.'

As the hammering and shouting continued in the courtyard outside, he led them swiftly to the far end of the room where there was a very high backed chair.

'Now,' said Father Andrew with the air of someone who is pleased with the surprise he is about to perform, 'Watch!' and he pulled the chair away from the wall to reveal a tiny door which he opened.

Davie gasped. 'Goodness! A secret passage!'

Their uncle nodded. 'Quick! In you go! The passage will take you down to St Fillan's Cave below the Priory. I'm afraid there isn't time for candles. You'll have to feel your way, so take it slowly. It's rather steep.'

He opened the door and pushed them in, then shut it quickly. They could hear the chair being pulled back again into place. The passage they were in sloped downwards and Davie groped his way nervously, a hand on the clammy wall at each side. It was pitch black.

'Careful, Lizzie, careful! I can't see a thing,' Davie kept repeating as he felt his way along. After a short while Lizzie became a bit impatient with him and snapped,

'Look, Davie, why don't I go first? This place is as easy to me as if it were in broad daylight. Remember, I live in the dark all the time!'

Her words took Davie by surprise.

'Why so you do, Lizzie ! All right! You go in front, but mind how you go!'

So Lizzie squeezed past him and went on ahead calling back to Davie to warn him when they came to a tricky bit. She was pleased for once to be the 'eyes' for her brother instead of always relying on him to see for her.

They came to a kind of stair where footholds had been hewn roughly out of the rock. There was no knowing how far down one might fall if one lost one's footing. They could hear water dripping down below and it sounded a long way off.

They climbed down and down into the damp darkness and after what seemed an age to Davie they reached a sloping earth floor.

'I think this must be the bottom, Davie,' announced Lizzie. 'Now what do we do?'

'Wait for Uncle Andrew.'

St Fillan's Cave

Lizzie felt around the cave. There were a lot of chests standing on the earth floor about them and out of curiosity she opened one. She gasped as she felt inside.

'Davie, quick! Come here!' she shouted.

'What is it? Where are you Lizzie?'

'Over here!'

Lizzie walked over to where Davie was and guided him over to the chest that she had opened. 'Look at this!' she said excitely.

'I'm looking', replied Davie impatiently, frustrated by the darkness, 'and I can't see a thing!' Then he remembered that Lizzie could not see anything either and he regretted immediately speaking so sharply.

'No, daftie! I mean feel!' said Lizzie excitedly and she placed what seemed to be some sort of goblet into his hand. Davie handled the object carefully. It was made of a heavy metal with much ornamentation and he could feel large stones or jewels set into it.

'Goodness!' he gasped. 'This must be all the Priory treasure, down here for safe keeping.'

50

Then they felt through all the chests. There were more cups — many more cups — and there were crosses and candlesticks, books and vestments, as well as a whole pile of carved statues. They would not have believed a Priory could have owned so much. So engrossed were they in their discovery that they were oblivious to everything else. It was with horror that Lizzie suddenly realised with her keen sense of hearing that they were not alone. Someone was coming down from the secret passage!

'Quickly!' she whispered to Davie. 'Someone's coming!' She grabbed him and pulled him to a hiding place behind one of the chests.

They squatted down as close to the ground as they could. Peering cautiously over the top of the chest, Davie was able to see only flickering candle-light which threw giant jumping shadows on to the uneven rock walls of the cave. There was no sound. In the uncanny silence Davie imagined that it must be Walter creeping down to find them. What had happened to Father Andrew and Brother John? Where could they run to from here? He glanced around panic-stricken but there seemed to be no way of escape. He looked again at the oncoming shadow dancing menacingly on the walls and was thankful that Lizzie was unable to see.

A black figure had now reached the floor of the cave and its eerie dancing silhouette reached right up to the roof. Davie cowered hoping that they would not be visible in the dim half-light. The footsteps were now coming nearer to the chest where Davie and Lizzie were hiding and then they stopped. Davie ducked down not daring to look up. He could hear his heart beating and his hands shook as he clutched Lizzie to him.

'Lizzie! Davie! Where are you?' a voice echoed out over their heads.

Davie and Lizzie gasped with fright.

'Goodness! There you are!' said Father Andrew in his kindly voice. 'Right beside me all the time! My eyes aren't what they used to be alas!'

Brother and sister staggered weak-kneed into his arms.

51

'Well, my children! I see you managed the secret staircase all right. It's not easy to negotiate if you haven't been down it before.'

'Where's Walter?' asked Davie worriedly, unsure of Father Andrew's easy going manner in the face of such awful circumstances. 'What's happened to him? Is he upstairs waiting for us?'

'Don't worry,' reassured Father Andrew. 'I've convinced him that I haven't given you any help — which indeed I haven't as yet.' His eyes twinkled mischievously. 'He said he was heading back home for the night but I suspect he may return in the morning unless he cools off on the way back to Crail. He knows that you couldn't have got far yet. It's time to think seriously what we are going to do with you two.'

Davie agreed. He had had enough excitement for one day and now only wished to get on with their journey and out of reach of Walter as soon as possible. Lizzie, not fully realising how much danger they were in, was disappointed to think that they would have to leave their uncle again so soon. Meanwhile Father Andrew was muttering almost to himself.

'I think your best plan would be to go to Earlsferry which is only a little way further along the coast. I shall take you there myself at first light tomorrow morning — the sooner the better — in case Walter should reappear on the doorstep. I know most of the boatmen there so we should be able to find someone who'll take you over the Firth. They're eager for all the custom they can get these days as the pilgrim trade to and from St Andrews has diminished drastically with all the troubles in the country.' He paused, as if pondering over the changes there had been since what he termed the 'good old days'.

'Is it a long way, uncle?' piped up Lizzie.

'What, to the other side of the Firth? No, it doesn't take long with a favourable wind. We'll be setting off early anyway because of Walter so you'll easily be there by nightfall.'

It all sounded quite straightforward and Davie was relieved but a thought suddenly occurred to him. 'How much will the ferrymen charge us to cross in their boats?'

'You're quite right to be practical, Davie,' said Father Andrew. 'How much money do you have?'

'Well none', replied Davie, 'as yet. I had planned to beg for alms as we went along.'

'Ah well! that won't do,' said the monk shaking his bald head solemnly, and the shadows thrown by the candle leapt round the cave as he did so. 'So many monasteries have been closed or abandoned that it's not so easy to do that nowadays. You certainly can't rely on them. What's more, there are now strict rules about begging on the other side of the Firth. You have to wear an official badge to be a beggar, otherwise you are liable to all sorts of awful punishments.' He did not expand on these for fear of alarming Lizzie.

'I have a string of amber beads,' said Lizzie gaily, 'which we could sell. The wise woman of Crail gave them to me a long time ago. They're said to cure blindness but they don't work.'

Father Andrew smiled at her gesture and patted her on the head. 'No, lass. It'll take a little more than that, I'm afraid! You keep them. I have treasure enough here to spare.' And he waved his arm over all the large boxes which stood in the darkness beside them. 'In these chests are all the valuables from the church upstairs. We brought them down to save them from the Reformers but I don't see any point in keeping them indefinitely. I'd rather see them being put to some worthwhile use than moulder away in this cave for the rest of time, or worse, fall into the hands of those Protestants. Now let me see . . .' He went over to one of the chests and kneeling down rummaged through the contents with one hand, holding the candle above it in the other.

After a short while he produced from its depths a package which turned out to be a small leather bag.

'This is what I was looking for,' he declared triumphantly. He stood up. 'Now then, let's go up to the Refectory again and the fire - it's a bit chilly down here.'

53

Arriving back in the Refectory, they pulled up three chairs to the fire and Father Andrew brought out the leather pouch that he had found in the cave below. He undid a thong which was tied round the neck of the bag and emptied the contents into his lap.

Davie gasped at the sight. There on his uncle's lap lay about two or three dozen gold and silver rings, some with jewels of all colours in them.

'Now,' said Father Andrew contemplating them, 'you are also going to need something to give to the clergy at the Well at Restalrig. I suspect that money will speak louder than words, so you had better go prepared.' He picked out a few of the rings into his hand.

'Some of these rings, it is said, belonged to St Fillan himself but I very much doubt it. He was too holy a man to be bothered with such frippery. I suspect that they are more likely to be of Viking origin. However . . .' and he paused and looked at Davie with a gleam in his eye, '. . .it would probably do no harm to tell the priests at Restalrig that the rings are said to have been worn by St Fillan.' He chuckled slyly. 'That's one advantage about the clergy of the Old Faith. They're very gullible about such things! Now I'll give you a few rings just in case you decide to stop at Restalrig for a while and need to pay for lodgings, but this one here . . .' and he held up a golden ring with intricately designed patterning. It gleamed in the dancing flame-light as both he and Davie were caught up in the mesmeric effect of its beauty. Lizzie, unable to appreciate the effect of the ring for herself, wondered what the pause was for.

'Well, Uncle Andrew, what *is* it?'

'. . . this one,' he continued, 'is the most exquisite. Keep this one to present to the priest at the Well of St Triduana.'

He tied a cord through the ring which he then placed about Lizzie's neck beside the amber beads.

'This is for you to carry, lass. If you should fall into evil company it is unlikely that they will look for riches on you. May it do for you what the beads could not! May it bring you the sight you seek!'

Then he gave Davie the handful of rings which he had picked out from the pile in his lap.

'These are for you laddie, to do with as you think fit.'

'But Uncle,' stammered Lizzie, 'you're giving away your precious treasure!'

'Och, away, Lizzie!' laughed Father Andrew at her earnestness. 'You're welcome to it! Besides, it isn't mine really for all the treasure down there belongs to the Priory. But,' he sighed, 'the Priory won't last much longer I'm afraid. There are few enough of us left as it is even if the Reformers don't burn the whole place down.' He looked dejected at the thought.

'But what will you do, Uncle?' said Lizzie, shocked as she suddenly realised how the Reformation was going to change her uncle's life. 'Where will you go?'

Father Andrew smiled, touched by her concern. 'Don't you worry about me child. The Good Lord will provide. At the moment it is you who are our worry. Now, where were we? Ah yes, now, we still need a little something for the ferrymen.' He gathered up the rest of the jewellery and tipped them back into the bag. 'There's plenty here. I'll see to that for you.' He rose to his feet. 'And now, my children, it is getting quite late. We must find somewhere for you to sleep. Come with me.'

So saying, Father Andrew led them out of the room and along a passage to a large circular stair. With his candle he guided them up into a room with a large wooden bed. Davie could not contain his delight having seen one only once before in St Andrews. Neither of them had ever slept in such a bed.

'It's a bedstead!' he exclaimed, 'with soft mattressing!'

'What's that?' asked Lizzie intrigued.

'Feel it, Lizzie,' said Davie guiding her hands over it. That's where we are going to sleep.'

Father Andrew smiled.

'This is the Abbot's; or was before he went off in such a hurry. You're welcome to it. I wish you a peaceful night.'

Neither Davie nor Lizzie would have believed how soft and comfortable it could be! Davie fell asleep straightaway but

Lizzie spent a restless night, tossing and turning from one dream to another.

First she dreamt that she was being chased by Walter, her step-father. She ran and ran and still he kept coming with heavy footsteps and dire threats and above it all she could hear the ceaseless sobbing of her mother.

Next St Fillan appeared, sitting in his cave, surrounded by all the chests of treasure and wearing the ring that Father Andrew had placed around her neck. He nodded benignly at her but said nothing.

Finally she lapsed into the usual nightmare with the intense blackness and the feeling of falling down and down. About her shot wild fiery sparks and writhing, leaping flames. Then there was the terrifying shouting and screaming all around as she lay helpless on the freezing ground while the ghoulish dark shadow came bending over her to carry her off. She awoke hot and exhausted from struggling to escape to the sound of her own screams and found Davie bending over her crying 'Lizzie, Lizzie!' as he tried to rouse her out of her nightmare.

'It's all right Lizzie. You're quite safe, quite safe.' He stroked her brow and spoke soothingly to her. 'Poor Lizzie! Don't worry, I'll watch over you. It's only your dream again. Try and go back to sleep. I'll be here.'

Exhausted, Lizzie soon fell into a deep and sound sleep and Davie watched her anxiously in the dim light of their room. His thoughts began to wander to the day ahead of them. They had to get away. They could not afford to spend any more time at the Priory. Walter, he was sure, would be back.

As dawn began to break he lay listening to the distant rustling of the sea and hoped that the weather would be favourable for their journey.

Across the Forth

They were both sound asleep when Brother John came to wake them in the morning. Although the monk's squint was still a little off-putting for Davie, he was much more affable towards them than he had been the day before.

'Come now, children, up you jump. You've lots to do and a long way to go. Come down as soon as you're ready.' He twisted nervously with the end of the cord that tied his habit and Davie guessed that he was still worried about the prospect of Reformers attacking the Priory - perhaps more so now that there was a fairly strong possibility of Walter returning that day.

When they went downstairs, there was a steaming bowl of porridge for each of them waiting on the dining room table. As they were eating Father Andrew appeared.

'Good morning both of you!' he said brightly. 'I trust you slept well.'

'Yes thank you,' replied Davie politely.

'It was so lovely and soft,' added Lizzie. 'We only have turf and heather at home which is much more spiky!'

57

She did not mention her nightmare, but Father Andrew noticed that she was looking tired and pale. He hoped the journey was not going to be all too much for her.

Davie, seeing his concern, tried to cover up by asking cheerfully, 'Well, Uncle, how is the wind blowing this morning?'

'Do you know this,' answered Father Andrew. 'It couldn't be more perfect! I think God is on your side.' He hesitated a moment. 'You're quite sure that you want to go ahead with this, Davie, are you? It's a long way to be taking a young lassie.'

Lizzie was aghast. 'Of course we have to go, Uncle. I won't be any bother to Davie, I really won't. I want to go so much.'

Father Andrew smiled wistfully at her fervent, ashen face.

'Anyway,' added Davie practically, 'there's Walter to think about as well. If we went back now our lives wouldn't be worth living so we might as well go on.'

There was indeed something in that.

'Well, well,' said Father Andrew, 'in that case hurry up and finish your porridge both of you and let's get going. Brother John has already gone down to the harbour to make ready the boat.'

He took them out through a side door and the morning was sunny like the day before with a fresh breeze blowing. They went through a gate in the Priory wall and down a steep path beside a sheer rock face. Father Andrew pointed it out to Davie and said quietly, 'Behind that rock is St Fillan's Cave where you hid yesterday.'

The harbour, when they reached it, was humming with busy people. As well as fishermen and fisherwives there were merchants loading cargoes of wool and dried fish. The tide was out, but unlike Crail, there was always a place to moor in water if one wished. Brother John had the Priory boat tied up now at the end of the harbour wall and Father Andrew led them quickly to the place.

'Here we are, children. In we get!' The harbour wall was quite high and it was necessary to climb down to the boat by a wooden ladder. Father Andrew went first with Lizzie, guiding her carefully down. The rungs were far apart so she was glad of

58

his helping hand to place her feet safely on each foothold. Davie followed them nimbly and ably. He was eager and excited now that the adventure really seemed to be starting.

Brother John cast them off and waved briefly, then turned back to the Priory. Father Andrew rowed skilfully away from the harbour scanning the sea-front all the while. He knew from the meeting with their step-father the night before that there was every chance the man would be back again combing the coast for them today. He was glad that they had even got this far without any sign of Walter.

It was indeed a lovely morning and out on the sea they felt safe as if at last they were getting somewhere. Father Andrew raised the sail and with the fresh wind behind them they moved at a steady and even pace along the coast. There were plenty of boats already on the water and Davie did worry about pirates. But pirates would surely not bother with a tiny craft the size of theirs. They passed the squat church of St Monan and on the cliffs nearby a doocot shone in the morning sunlight. In a short while they were passing the little village of Elie with its sandy harbour. Here Father Andrew took down the sail and began to row towards Earlsferry on the far side of the bay.

'Now,' he said, 'we shall put in here and see if we can find you a passage.'

It certainly looked hopeful. There were about half a dozen goodly-sized boats drawn up at the jetty. As they drew in and Davie prepared to jump for shore with a rope to make fast their boat, a swarthy man who had been busy working on a boat nearby came over to catch the rope for them and helped to pull them up on to the sand. It seemed that Father Andrew recognized him.

'Well now, if it isn't Jock Thompson. How are you doing, my good man?'

'No' bad, Father. Trade isn't great at the moment with the troubles but och, there's aye something. We've never died a winter yet. And yourselves? I hope you've no' been bothered at the Priory.'

'No, thank you, Jock. I expect the Reformers have bigger fish to fry!' the monk joked.

Jock took their rope and made the boat fast. He eyed up Davie and Lizzie. 'And who's this you've got here, Father? You're no' planning a rival ferry service of your own, are you?' The man laughed at his own wit.

Father Andrew smiled at him. 'Indeed not, you old rogue, but I have here two passengers for yourself, if you're still in the game?'

'Aye, I am that or at least I could be persuaded you might say.' He winked at Davie.

'Right then,' said the monk leaping out of the boat, 'let us go up to the hostelry and see if we can come to some arrangement.' He lifted Lizzie out and she walked up with the two men.

As they went Father Andrew explained quickly to Jock that Lizzie was a blind girl from Crail and was going on pilgrimage to Restalrig with her brother.

'Oh, aye,' said Jock, 'I've heard o' the place. There's been a fair few folk through here who've been travelling to Restalrig over our ferry. '

'Ah, well,' continued Father Andrew, 'they're also in a bit of a hurry. Their step-father, Walter, is very angry that they're going on this journey and is more than likely to come after them to try and take them back.'

'No' Walter Fisher frae Crail!' exclaimed the ferryman.

'Aye, that's him,' replied Father Andrew nodding. 'He's married to my sister Jeannie Cunningham.'

'Aye, we ken him fine here, we do,' said Jock with some fervour. 'There was a barney here last year when John Knox was trying to hire a boat to take him over to the Berwick coast on the other side of the Forth. Us lads weren't keen to get involved with the man as there was still many a shipload of French soldiers out in the Forth would have sunk us like a shot if they had found out who was aboard.'

Father Andrew nodded. It would have been true enough.

'Anyway,' continued the ferryman, 'Walter Fisher, who was among Knox's escort at that time, was mouthing it off to all and

60

sundry about us being wicked Papists. Needless to say a fight broke out between him and us boys from Earlsferry. Of course his single strength was no match against the whole lot of us and when he realised that we were getting the better of him he withdrew saying that he'd be back to settle his score with each of us separately. We haven't seen him since. John Knox got his boat from Pittenweem in the end.'

'Aye, I watched him go,' said Father Andrew, remembering the stir it had caused. Then getting back to the matter in hand he continued, 'So you'd be able to set off fairly soon would you?'

'Certainly, I'll need to get my mate Sandy out o' here,' and he nodded towards the hostelry which they had almost reached, 'but the tide's just right, we can go anytime.'

Father Andrew was relieved as they entered the door of the building. Things seemed to be working out for them.

Davie meanwhile was still down on the jetty. He kicked idly at the stones at his feet and gazed absent-mindedly out across the Firth. It was a fine day. If they could get a ferryboat it would be a quick crossing for there was a good breeze blowing. He broke out of his reverie to find himself alone. Brother John and Lizzie had gone off with the bronzed ferryman. He was about to join them when suddenly over the lapping of the waves beside him, he heard the pounding of horses' hooves. It was an unusual sound to hear in those parts and often meant that some dire news was being delivered. He strained to catch a glimpse of the horse and rider, and managed at last to spot them hurtling down the path to the ferry.

His curiosity and interest turned at once to dismay and horror as he realised that the rider was none other than Walter spurring his horse on like some frantic demon. Goaded into action by the shock, he ran up the beach to the inn, where he found Father Andrew, Lizzie and the man they had met on the beach engaged in lively conversation with a half-dozen or so other ferrymen who were obviously agog to hear where Lizzie was going, not least perhaps because of her relationship with Walter Fisher who of course they all knew well from their little fracas the year before.

61

'Och, we'll see you all right, lass,' one of the men was saying as Davie burst in. 'The man Fisher'll no' get past us.'

They looked round in surprise as Davie entered breathless from his haste.

'Quickly!' he shouted to the company and his eyes went immediately to Father Andrew, 'it's Walter! He's coming down the road! On a horse!'

Jock took command immediately, rising in one movement to his feet.

'Don't worry, son! Leave him to us.' He nodded to the rest of the assembly in the dark low-ceilinged room. 'You know what to do, lads!' He winked at them. There was a chorus of 'Aye, aye,' from the gathering like the rumbling of a distant storm. Jock beckoned to Father Andrew and Davie, 'Quick, come with me, this way. I'll carry the lass.' He whisked Lizzie off her feet as if she had been a feather pillow and made towards a small door opposite to the one they had come in by. Lizzie, bemused by the sudden rush, was aware only of a smell of sea and sweat together which overwhelmed her as Jock squeezed her close to him to get through the narrow door. Sandy, Jock's friend, brought up the rear and had only just closed the door behind them when the main door was thrown open and Walter walked in.

'Right!' he shouted, thumping his fist on a table, 'where are they, landlord?'

The landlord who was sitting among his guests raised his eyebrows in mock ignorance and replied as slowly as he dared, 'Where are who, sir?'

Walter was furious. He had seen Davie from the distance as he had come down the ferry road, now his face turned purple with rage as he drew himself up to his full height. 'Don't you try to play games with me my man, or I'll have your place closed down, - or worse!'

The landlord knew that Walter probably had enough Reformer friends to carry out this threat, besides which he reckoned that Ferryman Jock and his little party should have put out safely to sea by now.

'Very well then, sir,' he addressed the lean, angry man, 'you might do worse than try down at the jetty.'

Walter stormed out. 'You'll hear more of this, my man!' As he went the rest of the men in the room rose purposefully to their feet and followed him.

The landlord was right. Jock Thompson's boat had pushed out though there was only himself and Sandy to be seen busily rowing with strong even strokes. Davie and Lizzie were lying flat on the floor of the boat but Walter guessed they were there. He shook his fist at the receding stern.

'Just you wait till I catch up with you Davie Cunningham!' he yelled. 'You'll regret you were ever born, unless you change your mind now and leave the lass behind.'

Lizzie shivered at his threats from her hiding place and all she could hear was Jock's merry laugh ringing out over the water. Jock waved goodbye to Father Andrew, who was watching from the top of the jetty. Walter interpreted it as a mocking wave of triumph.

He was livid. He was not one to be thwarted. He stormed about offering to hire a boat from anyone at twice the normal price, but the stalwarts who had followed him from the hostelry stood around him menacingly in a circle with their arms folded. One of them spoke,

'None of us will hire you a boat, sir. You of all people should know the custom of sanctuary of the Earlsferry. No fugitive from this place may be pursued until he is at least half-way across the Forth. So settle yourself for a good wait, my man. They're hardly out of earshot yet.'

Indeed they were not. Walter turned back to the horse. 'In that case I shall go back for my own boat. No one gets the better of Walter Fisher.'

He mounted to the sound of jeering from the men who were standing around and set off in the direction of Crail without a backward glance. The sound of hooves could be heard clattering off into the distance.

Father Andrew turned to the men on the jetty.

'Well, that's that for the meantime anyway! Thank you all very much. May God reward you all. And now I must be getting back. It's a long row home!'

By this time, the ferry boat was well out to sea. Jock was watching the scene on shore intently and gave a running commentary to Lizzie and Davie as they went.

'It looks as though Walter is going back home,' he said. 'Perhaps he has resigned himself to letting you go.'

The sun was high in the sky by now but it was very breezy in the boat as the wind whipped round them and the spray splashed over their heads. Davie and Lizzie huddled together in the big blanket that their mother had provided.

'I wonder how Mother is faring,' said Lizzie, suddenly feeling very far from home.

The Black Shadow

The wind and the tides were with them and they made good progress across the Firth. It was approaching late afternoon when they arrived at Gullane on the other side. Davie looked longingly at the miles and miles of sand and dunes.

'Lizzie,' he exclaimed, 'there are sand dunes here just like St Andrews!'

'The snag with that,' said Jock who had overheard his comment, 'is that you will have to wade ashore. We can only get so far in with the boat as the tide is already on the way out.' When they had got in as close as they dared Jock left Sandy in charge of the anchored boat and jumped over the side into the water with Lizzie and Davie. The water was very cold but the sand was smooth and soft and Lizzie wriggled her toes delightedly so that they were sucked in by the sand.

Jock led them across the beach and through the dunes. Davie offered him one of his precious rings in payment for their passage but the honest fellow waved it aside.

'No, no! Away you go!' he said. 'Father Andrew has already

given me something to cover your fare plus a little extra to ensure you a night at the pilgrim guest-house here.'

Davie smiled. 'Trust him to think of everything!' Jock nodded. 'Aye, he's an awful man that for his generosity!'

Through the dunes from their landing place was the guest-house and Jock introduced them to the landlord and his wife, a homely, welcoming couple.

'Poor dear thing,' said the wife, Mistress Gullane, when she saw Lizzie looking pale and tired.

She led her upstairs and into a bedroom. 'Here', she said, guiding the girl, 'is the bed, and here, a bowl with a jug of water where you may wash yourself.'

'Thank you,' Lizzie murmured, embarrassed by all the attention. 'You are so kind to us.'

'It's what we're here for,' the landlady replied simply. 'When you are refreshed, my dear, come down and have something to eat. I'll send your brother up to show you the way.'

'Don't worry, I shall manage,' said Lizzie. 'I get used to new places very quickly.'

'All right, dearie,' smiled Mistress Gullane as she left the room. 'I'm sure you'll do nicely. But give us a shout if there's anything you need.'

Lizzie washed her face and hands and lay down on the bed to try it out. What luxury! Another bed!

She must have fallen asleep because the next thing she knew was Davie shaking her. 'Come on, Lizzie, wake up! The good lady has the food on the table!'

'Oh Davie! Where am I?' asked Lizzie in panic. Then suddenly the happenings of the day came back to her and she remembered where she was. She patted the bed and smiled.

'Imagine that Davie, another bed! Mother won't believe us when we get back and tell her all our tales.'

Davie laughed at her wonder but secretly thought how if Lizzie should regain her sight all excitements of this journey would pale into insignificance.

They went downstairs for their meal which was more than

ample for their needs. Their hosts were a jolly couple who loved having company to entertain. As it began to get dark, Jock Thompson took his leave.

'I'll away now down to the boat for the night and see how Sandy's getting on. Tomorrow we leave as soon as the tide will allow us.'

Davie was disappointed. His face fell. Lizzie echoed his feelings. 'Can you not stay here for the night?' she asked.

'No lass,' answered John. 'It would indeed be fine, but these are wild days and a man must guard his possessions. It would be easy enough for a robber to steal away an unguarded boat in the darkness on the night tide. But if you and your brother should return this way, it may be that our paths will cross again. Indeed I hope that will be. Goodbye to you both!' So saying, he left.

Davie and Lizzie sat at the fireside awhile, talking with Bob Gullane, while his wife sat spinning and carding her wool. They told him all their adventures since they had left Crail.

Lizzie felt drowsy in the heat from the fire and when Mistress Gullane suggested that she should go upstairs to bed, Lizzie agreed readily. Davie, however, stayed downstairs a little longer inquiring of his hosts which course of action they would advise him to take next. His original plan had been to go straight to Restalrig but he hadn't realised how quickly they would travel, for he had intended reaching Restalrig on St Triduana's Day, which was October the eighth. Now he realised they had a few days to spare. Would they find somewhere to stay, he asked his hosts?

Bob was not sure, but he knew that the nuns at Haddington had plenty of accommodation. Although it would take them out of their way a little, it would certainly be somewhere safe where they could stay for several days. In addition, the road directly to Restalrig from Gullane, along the coast, tended to be frequented by lepers, all banished from the towns and begging their living as best they could. One could recognise them by their dark hoods and capes which covered their faces and even their hands. They carried with them clappers to warn people of their presence and were not allowed to speak to anyone, but had to make use only of their rattles to beg alms.

'How awful for them!' said Davie. 'Where do they live?'

'The lucky ones live in hostels run by monks and nuns — there's a leper house here and there's also one at Haddington — but even these are beginning to get scarce with the Reformation. The rest live under hedges or in the dunes along the coast. Many of them die from cold during the winter, but who is to care about them? Nobody wants to know.'

'It's the way of the world,' said Mistress Gullane from her corner, shaking her head solemnly.

'Anyway,' said Bob Gullane brightly, in an attempt to change the subject, 'you'd be wisest to go to Haddington for a while at least. There's a good road and I'm sure you'd find others in whose company you'd be able to travel in safety to Restalrig. I'd stick together in a crowd if I were you. There's many a traveller come to an unsuspecting end hereabouts. The lepers can be a nuisance too. Best to ignore them, or they will persist in following you with those infernal rattles.'

Davie smiled his thanks. 'Right, we'll do that! Thanks for telling me.' He yawned, 'I think I'll go to bed now too.'

'Aye, laddie,' said Mistress Gullane, 'you've had a long day of it. You'll sleep tonight I've no doubt.'

She was right. It was morning before Davie knew it. He had been given a room next to Lizzie's and was most surprised when he went through in the morning to find her already up and gone. He rushed downstairs, worried that she might have had her nightmare again and become disorientated but she was not downstairs either. He was relieved to find her eventually outside the guest-house, leaning against a low wall.

Lizzie turned at the sound of his footsteps. 'Hello? Davie? Is that you?'

'Of course,' he replied, coming up to give her a hug. 'Did you sleep quietly last night?'

'Yes, fine thanks. No dreams at all. What a lovely place

this feels. It's so peaceful and smells lovely. Even the sea sounds happy.'

'Of course it is,' said Davie teasingly. 'It doesn't have to fight rocks here to reach the tide-line.'

Suddenly a puzzled frown crossed Lizzie's face. It was a look that Davie knew well. It always meant that there was something that she couldn't quite work out.

'Davie?' she began queryingly, 'every so often, I can hear an odd kind of rattling sound.' She paused, straining, hoping to catch it again, but there was nothing to be heard except the sound of the sea rolling and a lark high in the air above, singing its sweet song. Davie looked all round, but could only see dunes for miles on either side.

'CLACK-AK-AK-AK.'

'There it is!' burst out Lizzie. 'What is it Davie?'

Davie followed the direction of the noise and saw that it was exactly what he had suspected. A leper, black-hooded and menacing, was skulking in the dunes some distance away from them, but not far enough for Davie's liking.

'It's just a leper, Lizzie,' he said as lightly as he could while a chill shiver ran down his spine. 'Bob the landlord was telling me about them last night. They aren't allowed to beg for alms with their voices but have to use rattles, which also warn people off as they advance. That's one of the rattles that you are hearing. Bob says, if we ignore them, they will not trouble us.' He refrained from telling Lizzie about the evil-looking black hood and the dark shapeless garment which made the leper seem more like a wraith than a person. The fellow he had just seen had certainly given him a turn - a tall, dark, formless spectre which had glided much more smoothly and swiftly behind the dunes than he had imagined a leper would. It was very eerie but he said nothing to Lizzie. He was convinced then that they would certainly wait till they could find some travelling company before setting off for Haddington.

As luck would have it, another boat-load arrived mid-morning and on it was a travelling friar called Gilbert with whom

Bob Gullane was well acquainted. Since the troubles of the Reformation this friar had continued to travel the country preaching but had avoided any open conflict with the Reformers.

'I've nothing against them,' he said when he was introduced to Davie and Lizzie, 'but they tend not to want to debate points, merely to insist that their own view is right. There are pulpits enough for all in this country. Now I'm heading south to St Bathans Abbey, for what I hope will be a rest. It's not far beyond Haddington, so I shall be glad of your company that far.'

They set off gaily, and as they walked Davie and Lizzie told Friar Gilbert of their plans. How they hoped to reach Restalrig before the Reformers closed the place down altogether and how they expected that Lizzie would receive her sight again through the intercession of St Triduana.

'It will happen, won't it, Friar Gilbert?' said Lizzie, looking for reassurance.

'Well my dear,' answered Gilbert, playing for time and trying to hedge his bets. 'They say that if you believe enough, it will be so, and I have heard of many people being cured of various eye ailments, both wholly and partly, but . . .' He broke off as he struggled to find the right words.

'But what?' prodded Lizzie impatiently.

'But, for some reason that I do not know, not everyone is cured Lizzie. I don't want to dash your hopes, lassie, but sometimes it seems that God's ways are not always our ways.'

'It shall be done. I shall see!' declared Lizzie with a vehemence that surprised even Davie.

'We are going to do everything we can to obtain a cure for Lizzie's blindness,' said Davie quietly. 'If it doesn't happen straightaway then we shall wait on until it does!'

'Of course, of course,' consoled Gilbert, regretting what he had said. 'I wish everyone was as full of faith as you two. I do believe you will be cured Lizzie.'

For a while they continued in uneasy silence.

There were quite a few folk on the road, but all good Christian bodies, with a cheery greeting as they passed. Presently Davie was

71

uncannily aware that they were being followed but every time he looked back he could see nothing. He tried to shake the feeling off. 'Probably still expecting Walter to appear from nowhere,' he said to himself, but later on, when he heard the 'Clack-ak-ak-ak' of a leper's rattle he knew at once he had been right. Turning quickly, he caught sight of a long dark robe disappearing into some bushes at the side of the road. Although it was a long way off he felt quite certain from its swift smooth movement that this was the same leper that he had seen that morning near the guest-house at Gullane. He did not like it one bit but he remembered Bob's advice and ignored him. With increasing frequency they would hear the eerie rattle grating on the air and Lizzie would cling to Davie's arm.

'There's that leper again, Davie. What a horrible sound he makes.'

'Yes,' replied Davie, 'but he'll no' trouble us.'

'Look,' suggested Gilbert, 'let's leave him some food and then perhaps he will go away and leave us in peace.' He turned out his small purse which contained just one small dry piece of bread.

'I'll leave him this.'

'No! Don't be stupid, Friar Gilbert,' interjected Davie suddenly embarrassed by the friar's generosity. 'That's your last piece of food. Look, we have still plenty here as we have been given more meals along the route than we expected.' He took two of the bannocks out of their basket, and then on a sudden impulse the fish that he knew their mother had so ill been able to afford. These he laid on a rock by the side of the road. Then he turned round and shouted, 'Hey, there!'

There was no-one to be seen at first, but presently the dark hooded figure slipped out from the shadow of the bushes at the side of the road some hundred yards away. Davie shouted again and with an exaggerated movement pointed towards the rock where the food lay. Then they all turned and walked on. When they looked back they saw that the leper had already reached the rock and was nimbly stuffing the food into a bag as if he thought they might suddenly turn around and snatch it back from him.

'You are a thoughtful person, Master Davie,' said Friar Gilbert not realising that Davie had been shamed into parting with his food by his own generosity. 'May God reward you!'

Davie was not at all certain that it had not been a rather over-hasty gesture. He remembered the words of their landlord at Gullane and realised that the leper would probably now dog them all the way.

He shivered, and it was not from the cold.

The Road to Restalrig

Davie was right. The leper was still keeping pace with them as they drew near to Haddington. Every so often they would hear his rattle or look round only to catch a glimpse of the figure sidling along the road some way behind them. Why was he following them, Davie wondered. Was it merely for food or was there some more sinister reason? It did seem odd that crippled and sick as he must be, he was able to match their speed. Davie was glad that they had Gilbert with them.

Just outside the village Davie and Lizzie parted company with the friar. He would press on, he insisted, despite their pleas that he come with them to the Nunnery at Haddington for the night. He wanted to reach St Bathans by dark.

'But we shan't know a soul,' protested Lizzie, sad to be parting with the friar. Gilbert merely smiled, patting her on the head, and bade them goodbye in his pleasant kind of way.

Prioress Elizabeth at Haddington was a woman of the old school, and her rotund figure betrayed the easy life of luxury she had been living. She was a hardy and shrewd person but generous withal and she welcomed Davie and Lizzie with open arms - particularly when Davie presented her with one of the rings.

'Have you travelled far, my dears?' she asked benevolently. They answered that they had come from Gullane that day but that they had set out initially from Crail in the Kingdom of Fife.

'Crail?' she echoed with gusto. 'Well I'll be blowed! What a stroke of luck! Come in! I have a surprise for you!'

She showed them into a room where several people were sitting and they were indeed surprised. With astonishment Davie realised that here were most of the Crail clergy. It turned out that the Nunnery at Haddington was associated with the Kirk at Crail. When John Knox's sermon the previous year had caused the locals and general riotmongers to pull down and destroy all the church ornaments at Crail, the numerous clergy of that vast church had decided to leave the village, discretion being the better part of valour. They had therefore travelled to their sisters in God at Haddington, at least until things settled down they said. Here needless to say they still were and looking none the worse for their enforced exile.

It was a joyful reunion for everyone. The Crail clergy were pleased to see Davie and Lizzie and hear the news from their old village, but saddened to hear that the Reformers were so strict on the local people.

While he commiserated openly with the priests on the way things had turned out for them, Davie had to admit to himself that if they had really been so keen on Crail they could have stood their ground and stayed. Here instead they were a living example of all the Reformers found wrong and rotten in the church, wining and dining in style through the generosity of Mother Elizabeth and her nuns. How long before Walter got word of them being here and organised a heavy gang of Reformers to chase them on their way again?

At the thought of Walter, Davie wondered for a moment where he might be. Had he indeed gone back and chased after them in his own boat? So far they had travelled quickly and Walter would have been hard put to catch up with them.

But the prescence of of the leper on the road filled him with unease.

They had a good evening discussing old times. Davie told the company of his plan to take Lizzie to Restalrig to bathe in the miraculous Well. The priests admired his bravery they said, and Lizzie's. It put them all to shame, but they did not see what else they could do.

The Prioress said Davie and Lizzie could stay on as long as they liked and they were glad to be able to rest for a few days in the safety of the monastery. Here at least the leper them could not follow them. Surely through lack of food he would latch on to some other group of travellers.

'Besides,' said Isobel, a bright young nun and a sister of the Prioress, when Davie confided his fears to her, 'there is a Leper House in the village. He'll be looked after there and then go his own way.'

It was therefore with some concern that Davie caught a glimpse of a leper from time to time when he looked over the Nunnery wall. He felt somehow from its furtive movements that it was the same sinister leper who had followed them all the way from Gullane. Regretting bitterly now the impulse that had caused him to leave out food for the leper despite Bob Gullane's advice, he wondered if that could be the only reason that the leper should seem to be waiting wraith-like specifically for them. Once he almost wished it were Walter after them instead. At least Walter made a noise and you knew exactly where you stood with him.

At the approach of St Triduana's Day Davie began, with some trepidation, to make plans for their journey to Restalrig. He was told that it would take them the best part of a day and was relieved when at the last moment Mother Elizabeth persuaded one of the timid Crail priests to go with them.

'But I shall travel in ordinary clothes,' he said apologetically, 'just in case we run into any Reformers.' His name was Thomas Kinnear, he told them, and he was a cousin of one of the priests of the college church at Restalrig, so felt that he could well be an asset once they arrived there.

Davie was more than pleased to have him for the road. With that evil looking leper still lurking round there was some comfort in numbers.

It was the seventh day of October when they set off along the last lap of their pilgrimage — the road to Restalrig, well trodden by pilgrim and soldier alike since the days of the Romans. Davie and Lizzie were sorry to leave the Prioress and her Nunnery where they had been so comfortably treated, but were happy to be on the road and excited at last to be so near their goal.

Their excitement did not last beyond the first rattle.

'Clack-ak-ak!'

The leper picked them up as soon as they left Haddington. He followed more closely now and seemed even taller, darker and more menacing. He rattled his clapper almost incessantly.

'Well I'm not feeding him this time,' said Davie firmly. 'Bob Gullane warned us that we would never shake them off if we did and he was right.'

He looked to Thomas for his opinion but their travelling companion was non-committal.

'Don't be so hard on him, Davie,' pleaded Lizzie. 'He's going to follow us anyway making that awful noise so, since Mother Elizabeth gave us plenty of provisions, we might as well feed him and then perhaps he will at least follow us quietly.'

Davie realised that there was reasoning in her words.

'All right, Lizzie,' he said grudgingly, 'you may be right. I suppose if he must follow he may as well do it silently.'

Acting against his better judgement for the second time he reluctantly set out some food by the road as before and with a shout and a wave, indicated to the leper that he had done so. Then they pushed on and yes, Lizzie was right, the leper's rattle fell silent and so the journey was rather more pleasant than they had expected.

There were a lot of people on the road that day, for it led not only to Restalrig, but on to Edinburgh as well and beyond that to Stirling, one of the Queen's most important strongholds.

Occasionally they met people speaking a strange language that they did not recognise. It did not seem to be like the Flemish that they would often hear in Crail when boats came in. Thomas told them that it was French and that the speakers could well be some of the retinue of the Queen's mother, Queen Mary of Guise, who had recently died. 'Any day now, it is said they are intending to ship her body in it's lead-lined coffin, back to France.'

'And will the young Queen of Scots come to rule us then?' asked Lizzie.

'I doubt it,' said Thomas, 'for she is married to the King of France and that country is so much richer and more comfortable for royalty to live in than Scotland. But it's a pity. Without a Catholic ruler on the throne of the country, it's no wonder that the Reformers are doing so well. When, that is if, the young Queen Mary of Scotland ever comes, she is going to have to accept the New Faith as already established. Perhaps that will be the way of least bloodshed.' It was a topic that the priests had discussed a lot at Haddington.

The way seemed long today and Lizzie's feet were beginning to ache with the constant walking. She stopped and put on her shoes to make the road feel less hard. On either side the fields were empty and bare, many of the houses desolate and deserted. Davie wondered why there was so much barrenness.

'Earlier in the year,' explained Thomas, 'an English army came across the Border to attack Queen Mary of Guise's garrison of French soldiers at Leith, which is not so far from Restalrig. The Queen's men laid waste the countryside round about so that there would be no food left to sustain the enemy troops. What little they missed was soon taken by the English, who burned and pillaged the houses into the bargain. Now, although the two armies eventually made peace and withdrew, the people are wary of building their houses again so close to the road until they feel the country is a bit more settled.'

'I remember the siege of Leith,' said Davie. 'We used to watch the French and English ships sailing into the Forth from our cliff-top at Crail, didn't we Lizzie?'

'Aye!' replied Lizzie, 'and we used to hear the cannon firing over the water on calm days. It was fair scary!'

'And we used to see the smoke rising,' continued Davie, 'and knew that some awful battle was going on, but never found out until it was long over who had won the day.'

'You must have seen some fighting at Haddington in those days,' said Lizzie eagerly to Thomas. 'Tell us about it.'

Thomas shifted uneasily, glad that her blue eyes could not see his face reddening. 'Well yes,' he said hesitantly, remembering how they had all cowered in the Nunnery at Haddington while soldiers had set fire to the building. Fortunately the fire had never taken a good hold because it had been raining heavily at the time and Mother Elizabeth had discovered after that that if she handed out church treasures at intervals to the English captains, their soldiers would leave them in peace. 'We got used to having soldiers around all the time' Thomas added, not mentioning that these had been wounded soldiers that the Prioress had agreed to look after for the English army as part of the bargain.

'Look!' he said suddenly, relieved to be able to change the subject, 'there is the grand Kirk of Restalrig over there!'

Davie looked and saw an enormous church across the fields.

'Crivvins, Lizzie!' he exclaimed, whistling through his teeth in amazement, 'it's the biggest church I've ever seen! You wouldn't believe how big it is!' But Lizzie was not in the least bit surprised. It seemed only fitting to her that the church with the most famous Well in Scotland should be of extraordinary size.

She began however to feel rather nervous. The moment of truth was fast approaching now and she tried to push the doubts to the back of her mind. What if it didn't work? What if the Saints had no special powers indeed as the Protestant preachers said? Now that the hope had been raised, she wanted to see so badly that she didn't know what she would do if this pilgrimage failed.

She fell silent, depressed with excitement and anticipation, a knot in her stomach and a pain in her chest which made her feel breathless.

Davie was still enthusing about the size of the church.

'Of course it's big,' said Thomas. 'There are thirty-three altars in it.'

'Each with its own benefactor no doubt,' remarked Davie, 'paying good money to the clergy for prayers and Masses for their souls. That place must be worth a mint!'

Thomas Kinnear ignored the point which he felt was verging on the Protestant point of view.

'Over there,' he said, gesturing with his arm across the wasted fields, 'is where the vast army of English camped this last Easter.'

'It's a wonder that they didn't ransack the church of St Triduana,' commented Davie, 'being such a prime monument to the old ways of religion.'

'Aye, I suppose so,' agreed Thomas, but he suspected that the clergy of the College Kirk of Restalrig had probably had a similar arrangement with the army captains as the nuns had had at Haddington.

'We're nearly there,' he said. 'If we go round this side, you will see the chapel of St Triduana and the Shrine of the Holy Well.'

They skirted the outsize building and came upon a little hexagonal construction which though substantial seemed dwarfed by the size of the rest of the establishment.

'That's it!' cried Thomas admiring it. 'The Shrine of St Triduana! That building houses the Well where the miraculous water is contained and on the floor above is the Chapel.'

Davie gave Lizzie an excited hug. 'We're here Lizzie! We're here! We've made it!' and to Thomas he said 'How do we get in?'

'It's not so easy since the reforms,' answered Thomas, 'they're very wary here, as everywhere else, about letting just anybody in, but I have a cousin here so we should be all right. Come this way!'

He led the way round the side of the Chapel to a large house attached to the Church. There was a tall heavy door and Thomas knocked firmly with his hand.

At first nothing seemed to be happening, then a face appeared at a window above them.

81

'Go away!' said a frightened voice. 'We've no alms.'

'It's not alms we're looking for,' stated Thomas authortatively. 'We want to speak with one the of priests here, one James Kinnear'.

'He's not here!' said the face abruptly.

'Can I speak to someone in charge then,' asked Thomas impatiently. 'I am a priest of God myself.'

The face peered further out and said suspiciously, 'You don't look at all like a priest, if you don't mind me saying so.' Now Thomas regretted having left his clerical garb behind at Haddington.

They seemed to be getting nowhere so Davie spoke up desperately.

'Look!' he said, 'we are carrying a precious relic of the holy St Fillan from Pittenweem. If you will let us in we are prepared to bargain with it.'

'How do I know that this isn't a trick?' argued the face.

'It isn't!' pleaded Davie, but Lizzie pulled the ring still on its cord from under her shift and held it up in front of her.

'This is it here,' she said boldly. 'Come and look at it for yourself.'

At the first glint of gold the face disappeared from the window. The three travellers stood anxiously wondering what to do next when suddenly they heard the rattling of many keys within and the sound of bars being drawn. The door swung noisily open on creaking hinges.

The hallway was cool and dim and Davie was surprised to see a short man in front of them. He had assumed that the man at the window would have been taller.

'I'm sorry to have to cross-examine you like that,' he explained apologetically, 'but one has to be so careful these days. Now what can I do for you?'

'My sister here is blind,' answered Davie simply, 'and we wish her to bathe in the waters of the Holy Well.'

'I see,' said the cleric slowly. 'Let me see the ring.'

Lizzie brought out the ring once more and lifted the cord over her head. The man's eyes widened with astonishment as he eaxamined the intricate patterning in gold. He looked so long and hard that Davie eventually asked, 'Is it not enough?'

The man started out of his examination.

'Yes, yes, of course, of course,' he said vaguely, 'it'll do.'

'We would like the ceremony to be performed tomorrow upon St Triduana's Day,' continued Davie. 'Presumably you will be having grand celebrations.'

'Alas! No!' replied the priest sadly. 'We used to have a whole week of celebration. But the number of clergy here has dwindled drastically - many went over to France when the French troops went back after the Siege of Leith. There is only myself left here now and I have to keep a low profile with so many militant reformers about. But there will be a celebration of a sort tomorrow so you may bathe your eyes then, my girl.'

He tossed the gold ring in his hand then slipped it, cord and all, into a pouch hanging from his belt.

'You had better come this way,' he continued. 'No point in going away looking for lodgings at this time of the day.'

He took them along many passageways which felt cold, damp and unused and showed them into a small room with a vaulted ceiling. There were rows of benches on either side and arched windows high up in the walls.

'This is our Chapter House,' he said. 'You young ones may sleep here tonight. Father Thomas, if you are indeed the priest you say you are, you may come and spend the night in the clergy quarters.'

He swept Thomas out of the room and Davie and Lizzie were left in the gathering gloom.

They ate the last of the food that Mother Elizabeth had given them, then stretched out on the stone floor in their blanket and fell into a deep sleep.

St Triduana's Well

That night, Lizzie dreamed her nightmare again. Whether through tiredness or excitement, it seemed to be more real and terrible than ever before. The darkness was darker, the flames and sparks were brighter and more searing and the shadow that bent over her more evil and menacing. She woke up shrieking in terror and collapsed into sobs of relief as she felt Davie's arms around her.

'It's all right, Lizzie, it's all right. We're at Restalrig, remember? You're safe.'

She did not sleep for the rest of that night, but lay trying to banish the nightmare from her mind and thinking to the day ahead. She was exhausted by morning when Father Thomas came in with two bowls of steaming gruel.

'Now, children,' he said cheerfully, 'are we ready for the big day?'

Lizzie had put on her shoes for the occasion.

'What do we have to do?' she asked nervously.

'First Father William, the priest you met last night, will say Mass in the Chapel of St Triduana. Then we will go down and

84

bathe your eyes in the Holy Well with special prayers. That's all there is to it! As soon as you're ready, I'll show you where the Chapel is.'

They set off through various passages and corridors and at length came into the Chapel. For Davie there were two surprises there. The first was to see so many people. The Chapel was packed with folk, many of whom had obvious eye troubles.

'Who are all these people?' he whispered to Thomas.

'Mostly people who live near by. Some like you have come to seek a cure, others come each year to give thanks for a cure already received. Come! There is room up at the front.'

The second surprise for Davie was to see the ornate decoration of the Chapel. Burnished gold and silver seemed to reflect the candles of the altar on all sides. There were rich gold-embroidered drapes hanging on every wall and above the altar, laden with jewels of every description, a large gilded statue of St Triduana holding her eyes on a skewer for all to see. Round the statue's neck on its black cord, Davie noticed the ring that they had brought. He tried in a whisper to describe it all to Lizzie, but words were not adequate.

Then Father William and Thomas came in, in procession with several young boys, all dressed in exquisitely embroidered vestments, and the Mass began. As Father William droned on in Latin Davie realised that it felt a bit strange — it was quite a while since he had attended a Mass because of the Reformation.

For Lizzie, everything passed in a haze and it seemed no time till they were descending the staircase to the Well House beneath with the rest of the congregation. When her turn came, Davie guided her to the Well where she knelt down. Father William made the sign of the cross with a wettened thumb on each of her eyelids muttering some prayers in Latin that she did not understand. Then he handed her a ladleful of the water to drink. The water was sweet and cool, but with an odd kind of aftertaste that made Lizzie inclined to think it must be doing some kind of good.

But there was no blinding flash, no sudden vision! Lizzie did not see again!

She accepted it calmly. She had always kept a little spark of reservation at the back of her mind for just this very moment. But Davie was flabbergasted. It could not be! It had to work! His little sister had to get her sight back. He had staked everything on it and it had simply not occurred to him that it might not happen.

One by one all the other pilgrims left the Well House, till only Davie and Lizzie were left sitting on a stone step at the side, Lizzie trying to comfort Davie as well as she could. Father William went over to them.

'Come along now my children, you must go now!'

'No!' cried Davie, angrily, 'We can't go! Lizzie can't see yet. You can't have said the right prayers.'

Father William placed a hand upon his shoulder. He had seen this situation many times before.

'My son, sometimes these things take time and nobody knows the why or wherefore. Go away and keep praying every day. You'll be surprised at what may yet happen in God's good time.'

Father Thomas had decided to stay on at Restalrig, so they said their farewells to him and went out into the brilliant morning sunshine. Davie sat down despondently on the step at the main door.

'Perhaps it's true after all, Lizzie. Perhaps it is all idolatry and superstition. Perhaps the Reformers are right about everything and the whole business of pilgrimage is a big deceit.'

He paused, faced with the possibility of changing his whole way of thinking. 'What are we going to do? Where can we go? We can't go back and face Walter. Not yet anyway!' As he sat bleakly, gazing ahead, he suddenly noticed a black-cloaked figure huddled against the far wall of the church. He stood up angrily.

'There's that wretched leper again. Look at him! It's all his fault! It's him that's brought us this bad luck!'

'Don't be daft, Davie,' comforted Lizzie, putting an arm round his shoulders. 'Luck doesn't come into it. It's got nothing to do with that poor unfortunate leper at all.'

'You haven't seen him, Lizzie! I didn't tell you before, but he's clothed in black from head to toe, just like the dark shadow in the dream you keep having. He could be the very Devil himself.'

'Och, wheesht, Davie. You're imagining things now!' said Lizzie wondering how to cheer Davie out of his despair. 'We still have some rings left. Why don't we come back another day and try again?'

'Oh, Lizzie, Lizzie!' Davie smiled despite the cheerless situation. 'Always so optimistic yet look how life has treated you! Yes you are right. We'll come back another day I promise you. But where shall we go in the meantime?'

The leper's clapper rang out clearly all of a sudden.

'There's that confounded rattle again,' he complained, 'and we have no food to give him now even if we wanted to. Come Lizzie we'll have to move on. Let's go up to Edinburgh. Father had a brother once who was a weaver and came to Edinburgh to seek his fortune. If he's still there we may be able to find his whereabouts from the weaving community. If not we can find lodgings for a while and then go back to the Holy Well some other day. At least the leper won't be allowed to follow us into the city.'

Lizzie smiled happily. That sounded more like her big brother now! She was still blind but it wasn't the end of the world. She would cope well enough.

They came upon a milestone showing the road to Edinburgh. Not that one needed much guidance. As soon as they had climbed out of the hollow where the grand Kirk of St Triduana stood Davie could see the high silhouette of the Castle of Edinburgh on the skyline.

He looked round momentarily at the church that they had just left. It did not look so noble nor so grand now, lying below them with its spires and towers. He turned away in disgust, and squeezing Lizzie's hand tightly, set his face towards Edinburgh. Far behind he could hear the persistent clacking of the leper's rattle but even that failed to annoy him any more. Ignoring it he put his mind to describing the sights that he saw to Lizzie.

To their left rose a rounded green hill, and as they progressed he could see that on the Edinburgh side there was a shelf of sheer cliffs. To their right lay the loch of Restalrig, on one side of which could be seen a large house which had seen better days, surrounded by several large barns and a doocot.

'It must be the house of some noble-man,' explained Davie to Lizzie, with a mild surprise that it should have survived the ravages of the recent fighting in the area. 'Bribes again, no doubt,' he said to himself.

The road became busier the nearer they got to Edinburgh. As they climbed over a smaller hill they fell in with a pedlar who pointed out to them the Abbey that King David had built long ago. Kings who followed after, he told them, added to it and transformed it into a royal residence more civilised and comfortable than the draughty castle high up on its hill overlooking the town.

'They say that it's floored with gold,' added the pedlar in an intrigued tone, 'but I for one don't believe everything I hear.'

Soon they were caught up in a sea of people wending their way up the Canongate to the City Gate of the Nether Bow. They passed in with the crowds under the watchful eye of the guards. Davie held tightly to Lizzie's hand.

'Goodness it is busy,' he shouted to her. 'Must be Market Day!'

'Every day here is Market Day, laddie,' said a nasal voice behind them. A little sly man with a hunched back and a nasty scar on his face fell in beside them. Davie reddened, feeling foolish for having showed himself so publicly as the stranger he was. Ignoring the man he pulled Lizzie quickly after him and eventually found a quieter spot out of the mainstream of the crowd.

'Phew! That's better!' he said to Lizzie as the bustling and jostling around them grew less.

'This must be your first visit here!'

Davie turned, dismayed to find that the same shifty-looking man with the whining voice had followed them through the gate. When he saw the man's scarred, cunning face his hand went automatically to his pouch.

'Aye,' he said coldly, 'it is our first time here but don't worry, we've relatives in the town. We're not alone.'

Thankfully the man seemed to take Davie's point and sidled off.

'Who was that?' asked Lizzie.

'I haven't a clue,' answered Davie. 'An evil man looking to take advantage of us in some way no doubt. Come on, we'll walk around and at least look as though we know where we are and see if we can find any weavers.'

They set off up the road beginning to feel a weariness now after all the excitement of the day. Davie suddenly found his head pounding and his eyes watering but he said nothing to Lizzie as he led her along. He realised one thing, that the leper would not be allowed within the city wall and was glad that they no longer had to put up with his annoying rattle. And yet he still had the feeling that he was being followed. He shivered and pulled himself together. He was beginning to imagine things now, he told himself. The leper could not be in the town. The guards would not let him through.

They passed the weighing place and the Mercat Cross, the Cathedral of St Giles with its crown steeple, and the forbidding Tolbooth where so many miserable prisoners spent their last days before being hanged.

They stopped there and Davie looked around, uncertain which way to go next.

Someone tapped him on the shoulder. He turned sharply. It was the unpleasant little hunchback with the scarred face again.

'Lost are we?' he whined triumphantly and his face widened into a leering smile, showing few teeth.

Davie suddenly felt sick and terribly alone. He was lost in a town he did not know and the responsibility for his blind sister weighed heavily upon him. For a moment the whole scene swam before his eyes then he noticed with horror that the hunchback stranger was stroking Lizzie's long golden hair.

'Beautiful hair!' he was muttering. 'Beautiful hair! The lassie's blind isn't she? Why don't you sell the child to me? I can get her a licence to beg and then she will live comfortably with me for the rest of her life.'

Davie noticed with horror that the man was already gripping one of Lizzie's arms as if to make off with her. She winced unsure how to react.

'Help, Davie!' she cried in a little frightened voice and began to struggle.

Davie didn't know what to do. He pulled Lizzie quickly from the evil man's rough grasp and shouted, 'Run, Lizzie! Come on, run!'

Leading her by the hand they dodged between the people in the crowded streets — in and out, in and out — trying to escape. Every time Davie looked the man was following after them with an agility that was astonishing. On his own Davie could have easily outstripped him but Lizzie could not go so fast. He began to panic. The man's knowledge of the streets meant that he could anticipate their every move. Up and down closes and alleys Davie ran with Lizzie panting behind him. And each time he thought they were safe the leering face would appear again with its venomous cackle.

When Lizzie was completely exhausted and beginning to stagger on her feet, Davie suddenly realised that they were in the middle of a cloth market. Here were stalls and booths on every side, filled with goods of every colour of the rainbow. Here were the weavers all right and here if anywhere would be their father's brother. Davie looked madly at all the stalls. It was many years since he had seen his uncle, certainly before Lizzie was born and he did not see any weaver that he even vaguely recognised. He could see that the frightful man was closing in on them again and he searched wildly round. They had been climbing as they ran and were now almost at the Castle where the street ended. What on earth were they to do?

At the same time he looked up at the locked booths behind the market and was startled to see his own name in large letters above it. 'David Cunningham Cloth Merchant'.

90

Could it possibly be their uncle in such a grand shop? There was no time to ponder the coincidence and Davie decided to take his chances. Lizzie could go no further.

'Come on, Lizzie!' he urged, 'In here!'

They tumbled panting into the doorway.

Entering the shop was like entering into another world. From the rush and turmoil outside they fell into a deep calm and muffled atmosphere. The little room was hot, stuffy and dark. All round the walls, on shelves, lay bales and bales of different kinds of cloth. Behind a long counter, in the dim light, stood a severe-faced, but handsome woman, who was not at all pleased to see such scruffy looking travellers in her shop, especially travellers who looked as though they might be running from the law.

'What do you want?' she asked primly addressing Davie.

'Is this the shop of David Cunningham?' he gasped breathlessly.

'Indeed it is, laddie, and if you don't state your business quickly and be off, I shall get the Master himself to you.'

'Good,' said Davie drawing himself up as he recovered his breath, 'it's the Master that I wish to see.'

'Oh! Is that so? And just who do you think you might be?'

'Why! I'm David Cunningham!' said Davie smiling at the woman who obviously thought he was being insolent. Lizzie laughed, but then she could not see the woman's face twisting with fury.

Finally, the shopkeeper exploded. 'Get out! Get out you good-for-nothing scallywags! This instant! And don't you ever dare to put foot inside this shop again. I'll teach you to make a mockery of me.' And yelling, she deftly grabbed an iron poker from the fireplace and began to wield it at the sorry pair.

At the back of the shop there was the sound of a heavy curtain being drawn back and into the room stepped a large man.

'Now what's all this going on?' he boomed.

'It's a couple of cheeky blighters who won't leave.' replied the woman recovering her composure at his appearance.

91

The man turned to Davie. 'Now then young man what is the meaning of all this? Quickly or I shall march you down to the Tolbooth myself.'

'I'm sorry, Sir. I didn't mean to be rude. I was in fact telling this good lady the truth. I *am* David Cunningham and we are looking for our uncle of the same name.' And he knew straightaway looking into the eyes that were as blue as Lizzie's that this was his uncle standing before them.

Then there were tears and apologies all round and Davie explained quickly about the man who was chasing them.

'Show me him,' said Mister Cunningham, 'and I'll have him arrested for loitering!' But when they went to the door of the shop he was nowhere to be seen.

'The scoundrel will have disappeared fast no doubt when he saw where you came. I am a man of some importance in this town now and few would dare meddle with me.' He looked at them closely. 'Well, well! Robert's bairns! This is a surprise! You both look worn out! Come up to the house and we shall catch up on the news of the years!'

There was a staircase outside the shop which took them up to the living quarters. They were splendidly furnished. Davie noted soft woven rugs lying on the floor. There were also tables and chairs and a dresser on which stood several pewter cups. Their uncle must be quite a rich person!

'I was fortunate when I first arrived in this town,' said the merchant reading Davie's thoughts as he watched his amazement at the furnishings. 'The rules about craftsmen setting up weren't so strict then as they are now and I managed to find a share of a booth with an elderly weaver. When he died I inherited it and as the years went by, I began to employ apprentices until I found that there was no need for me to weave at all. I was now free to set up my own merchant business, trading with the cloth my own apprentices produced. I stopped weaving completely myself since a merchant may in no way lay his own hand to any craft. It's a regulation in the city. From there I have prospered and now have this thriving shop and a good business trading across

92

the sea to Holland. Now then, tell me! What is your news? What are you doing here? How are your father and mother? And who is this charming little lady here with the Cunningham eyes?'

Lizzie blushed and smiled shyly.

'This is Lizzie, my younger sister,' explained Davie simply. 'She is blind and Father is dead. He was drowned many years ago.' And he proceeded to tell his newly found uncle all about that fateful night when Lizzie had lost her sight.

The woman from the shop turned out to be the merchant's wife, Mary, and she joined them from the shop below. Now that she was not on the defensive, her face seemed softer. When she smiled, Davie would say that she was even beautiful.

'Well now,' she said, taking command of the situation, 'you both look tired and hungry. No wonder I took you for beggars. I expect you'll tell your story the better for a full stomach.'

She was right. As they ate plateful after plateful of meat and broth, Davie told the whole of their story from the beginning when the idea of a pilgrimage had been formed to that very morning when it seemed to have come to an abrupt end.

Mister Cunningham listened closely. 'I always suspected those clergy were up to no good,' he declared when Davie had come to the end of his tale. 'I've joined the Protestants now. One had to if one wanted to stay in business. Mind you, I don't suppose we're any better than the Catholic clergy we condemn. Like them we merchants realise on which side our bread is buttered.'

He drew up a couple of chairs beside the fire and indicated to Davie to join him. Davie was not sure whether it was the unaccustomed amount of food he had just eaten or the wine that his uncle had been distributing so liberally, but he felt heavy and hot and his head was pounding again as it had been earlier.

Fever and Fire

By morning, Davie was worse and lay in his bed tossing and turning in fever. Mister Cunningham was worried that it might be one of the dreaded illnesses such as smallpox, typhus or the plague. By law, every householder had to report if anyone in the household caught such a disease and failure to comply with this regulation brought severe punishment, usually branding with a hot iron on the cheek. To a man of David Cunningham's standing such a possibility was unthinkable. If he, David Cunningham, Merchant of Edinburgh, were caught harbouring a seriously ill person, it would mean the certain end of his business even if the rest of the household survived.

On the other hand to admit to one of these illnesses meant banishment for the sick person and a certainty that even if he did not have a serious disease, he would be herded out of the city with those who had and then it would only be a matter of time before he did catch some fatal infection.

Faced with this dilemma, David Cunningham talked it over with his wife and she, brave woman that she was, agreed to nurse young Davie herself. No-one knew that they had any visitors in the house so it should be easy to keep Davie concealed.

For three weeks, Davie lay in his fever while Lizzie sat patiently at his bedside, wiping his brow gently with a dampened cloth and trying to quieten him when he cried out in his frenzy.

While she sat, Lizzie worried. What would she do if Davie died? Suddenly the whole Restalrig trip had changed from adventure to nightmare. The only consolation was that they had found their relatives. What if Davie had taken ill when she was still in the hands of that evil man who had chased them? The thought didn't bear thinking about!

Then suddenly at the end of the three weeks the rasping in Davie's breathing stopped all of a sudden. Lizzie sitting alone beside him became alarmed at the change and rushed for her aunt.

'Quick! Quick!' she shouted, 'Davie's lying very still and breathing very low.'

Mary Cunningham came running through at once. 'What is it?' she cried and bent over Davie intently. For a moment she looked carefully at his cheeks then felt his brow with her hand.

'Oh!' she said, hugging Lizzie, 'he's sleeping normally. The worst is over.'

There was great excitement in the Cunningham household that night at his recovery. From then on Davie was back to his usual self again, though he was very, very thin.

'We'll have to fatten you up again,' said Mistress Cunningham cheerfully. And they were all pleased that the affair had ended so happily.

Davie was shocked to learn that they were now into November. 'We must go home, Lizzie,' he said. 'Mother will think that we have come to grief along the road.'

'Don't worry, Davie,' his uncle reassured him. 'I've sent a message to your Mother that you're safe with me. You're certainly not fit to travel in the state you're in.' Davie smiled reluctantly. His uncle was right. He did feel so tired and weak.

The month of November passed pleasantly enough. Davie would spend his days sitting by the window of the Cunninghams' house, telling Lizzie all he saw below - from the pigs snorting their way through the rubbish to the fine ladies picking their way delicately over the gutters, bags of sweet smelling herbs held to their faces to disguise the smell of rotten filth beneath their feet.

By the beginning of December, Davie was beginning to feel much stronger and he decided that they ought to attempt the journey home before Yule. 'We could go back by way of Restalrig to visit the Well for one last time,' he told Lizzie.

'You're wasting your time, nephew,' scolded the merchant, and Davie thought secretly that he was probably right, but he said to his uncle,

'We must visit the Well just once more for the sake of Lizzie! I promised her.'

His uncle resigned himself to it, but told them to come back again to him afterwards and he would find them a boat at Leith to take them all the way back to Crail. Davie was relieved. There would be no worries then about the return journey. They began to plan for their second visit to the Well.

The day before they intended going there was a proclamation at the Mercat Cross. They had heard the bell ringing and had put up the shutters on the shop to go and hear the news. It transpired that Mary Queen of Scots' husband, the King of France, had died.

'What will it mean?' asked Lizzie.

'It means,' said their uncle grimly, 'that she is now more than likely to return to Scotland and that will mean even more unrest between Catholic and Protestant I'm afraid. None of it good for business at all.' And he shook his head soberly.

The next day as Lizzie and Davie headed for Restalrig everyone along the road was speaking excitedly about the news. When they reached the Kirk of St Triduana it was Thomas who opened the door to them.

He was pleased to see them.

'I am glad that you have managed to come back,' he said welcoming them at the door. 'Have you heard the news? They

96

say that Mary Queen of Scots will come back and sit on her throne here now. Then the Old Faith will be restored and everything will be as it was.'

Davie shook his head. 'Our uncle in Edinburgh says that there will only be a lot more fighting and bloodshed if the young Queen returns.'

He produced a ring from his leather purse and showed it to Thomas. 'We've come to try the waters of the Well again.'

Thomas smiled, 'Right, I'll go and find Father William.'

In no time at all it seemed, Father William came bustling back, this time with a genuine welcome on his face. He took the ring from them immediately and then led them to the Well House and Chapel.

'We'll have a few prayers in the Chapel,' he told them, 'and then the ceremony at the Well.'

Davie found it strange to find the Chapel now empty of people. The candles on the altar were unlit and the gold and silver did not shimmer so richly, but seemed dull and lifeless. He looked at the statue of St Triduana above the altar. The 'Ring of St Fillan' which they had brought the last time had gone - traded for food maybe or a bribe to keep Reformers away?

He came out of his reverie to find that all the prayers had been said. Father William led them down the steep staircase. He bathed Lizzie's eyes for a second time with the water from the Well and gave her a ladleful to drink. Again there were no blinding flashes but Lizzie felt a certain peace afterwards and was loath to leave.

'Come on! Lizzie,' urged Davie, 'we must go now or we shan't be back at the Gate of Edinburgh before it closes for the night. The nights are so much sooner at this time of year.'

They walked back slowly, hand in hand.

'It isn't true, is it?' said Lizzie. 'The Well isn't miraculous at all!' She fought back her tears. 'Or perhaps I don't believe hard enough in it.'

'Don't be silly, Lizzie,' replied Davie. 'No-one could have believed harder in it than you.'

97

The next day their uncle, the merchant, hired a horse and cart to take them down to the Haven of Leith where his ship was waiting. Edinburgh was busy, for the first General Assembly of the new Universal Kirk, as they called the New Faith, was in progress and large crowds were thronging into the town looking for fun and excitement, many for trouble. John Knox was also in town and had been preaching against the total destruction of church buildings. In vain it seemed he was trying to curb the enthusiasm of the mobs for burning churches. They would need the buildings for their new Universal Kirk, he reasoned. It was only the statues and monuments of idolatry that were to be destroyed.

It was afternoon by the time Davie and Lizzie reached Leith with their uncle. Mister Cunningham pointed out a large vessel at the quayside. It was painted in a soft red colour and had the name *Golden Lily* written in gold letters across its bows above which the painted figure of a lady rose with carved streaming hair holding a golden lily in her hand. Davie could not help noticing how similar the figure was to the image of St Triduana in the Chapel.

'This is my ship, my children,' declared the merchant proudly. 'I bought her from the English.'

'What a beauty!' exclaimed Davie in admiration.

'I shall introduce you to the Captain and then I must take my leave of you. There is a lot of extra custom in the shop today with the the General Assembly taking place and I must go and help Mary. Promise me though that you will come back again to visit us.' They promised, and he took them to meet the Captain, James Scott, a young man with a competent air about him.

'Here are your charges, my Captain. Look after them well.'

'Certainly, Sir,' replied the gallant young man. 'I shall treat them as if they were my own children.'

They said good bye to their uncle and climbed aboard.

The Captain told them they would not be sailing till first light next day, but that they had the freedom of his ship until then. They walked around it and Davie saw that the holds were full of bolts of finished cloth as well as raw wool.

The early winter evening was beginning to set in when a messenger came running into Leith.

'It's the Restalrig Kirk! St Triduana's!' he shouted. 'They're burning it down!'

Davie jumped up and sure enough, above them, up the slope and through the gloom he could see thick black smoke beginning to rise in the direction of Restalrig.

'What's happening?' he shouted in despair.

Captain Scott had been speaking with the runner.

'It seems,' he said, 'that the Assembly has decreed St Triduana's Kirk a place of idolatry and superstition and has ordered it to be utterly demolished and rased to the ground.'

'Oh! No!' cried Lizzie horrified. 'They may be right about the idolatry, but what about poor Father Thomas and Father William? We'll have to go and rescue them, Davie.'

'Yes,' agreed Davie, 'you're right. They'll tear them to pieces. Can you wait, Captain, and we'll see if we can fetch the two priests to safety. They could come with us.'

'Are you two completely mad?' cried the Captain, not believing that he could have heard aright. 'You'll be trodden underfoot by that rabble! Can't you hear the roaring from here? It's the same folk that follow the Protestant preachers all over the country. They're only out for trouble!'

'I don't care, I'm going! We can't leave the poor priests to face that lot,' protested Davie.

'And I'm coming too!' declared Lizzie stubbornly.

Captain Scott was dumbfounded. 'If you take yon poor blind lassie up into the middle of that lot then you're an even bigger fool! I wash my hands of you completely and will not be responsible to your uncle for your actions if you leave my ship!'

At his words Davie swithered as to the advisability of taking Lizzie, but decided in the end that it would be better for them not to separate. 'We'll be back before long, don't worry!' he shouted to the concerned Captain as they hurried off the ship.

Captain Scott gazed after them helplessly, too concerned with how he would explain things to their uncle to notice a tall, dark

100

cloaked figure slip stealthily out of the shadow of a nearby warehouse and follow the two young folk in the fading daylight.

Davie and Lizzie ran up the hill, the shouting growing rapidly louder as they went. Soon they seemed to be among people who were running in all directions, many, Davie noticed, clutching gold and silver objects from the Chapel. By the time they got near darkness had fallen and the fire seemed to glow more brightly for it. They could feel its heat now and Davie pushed his way through the crowd, tears streaming from his face.

The shouts of hatred all around them were bloodcurdling.

'Father Thomas! Father William! Where are you? What have they done to you?' he shouted above the noise as he saw the scavenging rabble silhouetted against the flames in front of him.

He managed to locate the Well House and discovered in the gloom that the outside door had been smashed. He pulled Lizzie in after him. The Well was still trickling but the heat from the fire was turning the water to steam.

They raced upstairs where Davie found the Chapel stripped of all its former glory, and Father Thomas sitting sobbing uncontrollably holding Father William in his arms.

'Quickly! Come, Father Thomas!' cried Davie in horror when he realised that Father William was dead. 'You must leave him and come! You have to get out!'

'They've killed him,' was all the poor man could sob, over and over again.

'Aye,' replied Davie curtly, 'and they'll kill you too, if you don't get away from this place right now!'

Too late! A band of ruffians appeared in the doorway, with large wooden cudgels. They flung Lizzie to one side and she fell out of the doorway and down the steep stairs. She cried out and Davie started forward shouting 'Lizzie, Lizzie!' but a heavy hand on his chest stopped him from going to her. The leader raised a cudgelled hand to strike Davie, but a small man at his elbow nudged him and Davie saw with horror the evil leer of the hunchback who had chased them on their arrival in Edinburgh.

'Don't do that,' he urged his leader with his whining voice. 'Let's take them up to the Tolbooth so that they may hang or burn in public as an example to all. Then many will be able to enjoy watching them die!' He was rubbing his hands together in anticipation, his face stretched into a toothless grimace from ear to ear made even more gruesome by the flickering flames. There was a horrible cackle of evil laughter from the rest of the gang as they voiced their agreement to this suggestion.

Davie was stunned by the man's words and felt weak at the knees. He stumbled as he was pushed roughly towards the stairs. All he could think about was Lizzie. What would she do without him? Where indeed was she now? He looked round anxiously to see if he could see her.

To his horror he saw her limp body at the foot of the stairs and the black cloaked form of a leper bending over her. Somehow he knew it was THE black spectre who had followed them all the way from Gullane waiting for just this moment. Now whatever his evil intent, he had Lizzie in his grasp and was already condemning her to a slow living death by leprosy. He, Davie, was powerless to help.

A rough hand pushed him on, out into the roaring crowd and the frosty night air on which the terrible stench of burning was carried. He had lost sight of Lizzie.

Rescue!

Lizzie felt herself falling down and down. She seemed to bang her head on every stair but there was nothing she could do. The horror of the situation had left her quite helpless and she didn't know where she was.

Then suddenly she realised that it was the nightmare of her dreams becoming terrifyingly real — the darkness, the shouting, the flames and sparks.

It was *really* happening to her!

She screamed and could hear Davie's voice above everything else shrieking, 'Lizzie! Lizzie!' but was powerless to answer him. Then she was aware in her terror of a dark shadow bending over her and screamed again. She looked up. And she looked again. She was *seeing*!

A tall man in dark robes was carrying her gently in his arms out of the Well House. The crowd noticed him and drew back to let him pass. Outside, in a state of shock, Lizzie, completely mesmerised, looked around her unsure now whether she was dreaming or not. She saw flames leaping up into the air and — yes — the stars above! Davie had told her often

103

how they had twinkled in the night sky. Now she saw them for herself!

The dark man ran and ran with her, saying not a word till they were well away from the hubbub of the crowd. Her energy spent, Lizzie found she no longer had the strength to scream but when he eventually bent over her to put her down, she heard the familiar rattle of a leper's clapper from beneath his robes and she gasped in alarm. She realised now that this was a leper just as Davie had described. Maybe even the very one who had been following them all the way from Gullane. She began shaking with fear again but was powerless with shock to run.

'Wheesht!' the leper ordered gruffly. 'It's all right!' Lizzie's long years of blindness had trained her ears well and she recognised the voice immediately.

'Walter!' she exclaimed in disbelief, before fainting.

When she came to she found herself in a bed in a room with all sorts of strange objects. A figure walked into the room.

'Hello, dearie!' said the person kindly and Lizzie knew at once by the voice that it was Mistress Cunningham. She could say nothing but looked and looked till Mistress Cunningham could stand it no more. 'Well?' she said laughing and crying with joy as she came forward to hold her niece in her arms. 'Am I better or worse than you imagined?'

'I don't know,' replied Lizzie bemused, 'nothing is how I imagined it would be.' She tried to sit up and realised that she was very stiff and sore. 'Ow!' she said out loud.

'I'm not surprised,' said the merchant's wife fussing round her. 'Walter says you came down those stairs like a sack of tatties! You've slept like a log the whole night.'

The stairs! Walter! Then Lizzie remembered what had happened. 'Davie!' she cried. 'Where is he?'

'It's all right, my dear. Now keep calm. He's in the Tolbooth at present along with your friend Thomas Kinnear, but still alive and probably safer in there than in the hands of the mob gathered outside. Listen! You can hear the jeering from here!' Lizzie shivered as she heard the roaring of angry people shouting outside in the street.

'But what's going to become of him? Will they hang him — or burn him?' She shuddered in anguish as the thought crossed her mind.

'Don't fret yourself, lassie.' Mistress Cunningham gave her another big hug. 'Your uncle is a loyal Protestant Merchant with some say in this town. He's away down to the Tolbooth at present to see if there is anything at all that can be done about Davie and your friend the priest.' She hid her own fears that even David Cunningham might not be able to dissuade the unruly mobs bent on making Davie, and perhaps Father Thomas too, into public examples. Changing the subject she added cheerfully, 'And now, if you are feeling well enough, there is someone to see you.' Another taller person walked into the room and Lizzie smiled shyly wondering who this might be.

'Hello, Lizzie!' The voice! It was Walter! Looking not at all as she had expected him to be.

'Walter!' she exclaimed uncertain what to say to him. He came over and gave her a big hug and sat down on the bed beside her.

'Lizzie! How are you?'

Lizzie peered at him for such a long time without replying that he asked laughingly, 'Is there something wrong, lassie?'

'No,' said Lizzie simply without taking her eyes off him, 'I thought that you would look a lot crosser. Aren't you angry with us for running away to Restalrig?'

'Aye I was,' replied her step-father. 'I was furious with you when you escaped from under my nose at Earlsferry but I rode back straightaway for my boat. I had to guess that Jock the Ferryman would land you at Gullane and as it turned out I was right. On the journey over I had time to cool off and think things out and I decided that merely whipping you and possibly turning Davie out of the house was not going to be punishment enough for the disgrace that you had brought upon me. So I decided on

105

another plan. I would follow you at a distance and find out who gave you assistance along your road and then report them all to the Reformers to deal with publicly. I thought that that would be a far worse penalty for the two of you to know that you had caused your friends such suffering.'

'Crumbs!' said Lizzie taking in the full horror of Walter's plan. 'And did you do it?' she asked in a little timid voice, thinking of the nuns at Haddington who had been so kind to them.

He shook his head. 'No, Lizzie, I didn't in the end as it so happens. Och, I was keen enough at the start and I found a leper's rattle washed up on the beach at Gullane. That's what put it in my mind to dress myself as a leper. I managed to buy some dark robes off a pedlar and thought it was the perfect disguise. No-one would come near me to ask awkward questions. What I hadn't reckoned on was hunger. Real lepers can get food at the various leper houses in the villages but I couldn't risk that for fear of catching the disease. So I had only my rattle to depend on for begging for food.'

'It's a good job then that we left you some,' said Lizzie genuinely concerned.

'Aye,' replied Walter, 'it was. You know I've never seen eye to eye with your brother, especially with his going to college instead of coming on the boat with me. I can assure you though that I have never been more grateful to anyone in my life than I was that day when he left out the smoked fish. Och, I still followed you but the kindness of the food took the edge off my wrath. When you were several days in the nunnery at Haddington I thought at times I might die from hunger but then you came out and left out some more food for me. That was what finally changed my mind. How could I punish you after such generosity?'

'But what happened to you when we came into Edinburgh?' asked Lizzie curiously. 'You couldn't have followed us there, so where did you go?'

Walter smiled. 'Simple, Lizzie! I just took off my leper clothes and came into the city too. I lost you at first but I went to stay with John Knox who I met at Crail last year. He's

106

the minister at St Giles here now. He was interested to learn of what was happening at Crail since his rather lively sermon there last year.'

'And was it his sermon that roused the crowds to burn down Restalrig?' asked Lizzie as the memory of yesterday's goings on returned to her.

'Mercy, no!' exclaimed her step-father. 'Mister Knox is not a violent man at all. He's a man with a mission, certainly, and no time for what he calls superstition and idolatry but he doesn't agree with out and out vandalism. No, it was some other person's speech at the Assembly that got everyone going.'

'And is the Kirk at Restalrig completely burnt down?' asked Lizzie.

'They say so, though I heard a rumour that the Well House still stands - at least in part. Yours may not be the last miracle there!'

'Yes, it was a miracle wasn't it,' said Lizzie quietly, remembering the awful events of the day before and wondering at the change in Walter that could bring him to even admit that the return of her sight might have been miraculous. 'Though it didn't happen in the way I imagined. Can you help me to the window? I want to see all the things that Davie used to tell me about.' When she mentioned Davie she frowned remembering what had happened to him. 'Do you think Uncle David will be able to rescue him?'

'I hope so! All I know is that if anyone can save him David Cunningham can. He seems to hold a lot of sway in this town.'

Walter led Lizzie to the window and she looked down expecting to see the pink pigs and the ladies with their herb bags that Davie had so often described to her. Instead all she could see in the bright frosty air was an angry mob standing beneath them shouting and shaking their fists. They were picking out rotten vegetables from the stinking piles of rubbish in the gutter and throwing them at Mister Cunningham's locked booth beneath. At that very moment there was the sound of hurried footsteps on the stairs and David Cunningham appeared in the room.

'Uncle David!' Lizzie cried, 'I can see! I can see! The miracle happened!'

The merchant hugged her briefly then spoke quickly to Walter. 'I don't want to alarm you, but I think it wise that you leave as soon as possible. I've managed I think to arrange a ruse to save Davie but the crowd is not pleased as you can hear. You must get out of here! I have given orders for a horse to be waiting for you at the far end of the Nor' Loch. You'll have to leave the house by the back way and go down to the shore of the loch. From there you can make your way along to the east end where my apprentice Neil will be waiting with the horse. Then you may take the road to Leith where Captain Scott is still waiting patiently aboard the *Golden Lily*. Now this time you *must go* whatever happens. I cannot impress it upon you too much. It is not safe for you to stay. Walter, surely with you they will do as they're told and stay on board ship!'

Walter smiled grimly. 'Not necessarily I'm afraid, but don't worry, I'll do my best.'

The merchant's wife put together some food and warm clothing for the journey. 'There you are!' she said anxiously. 'Now you must go!'

It was beginning to get dark by now and the mob outside were more subdued, gradually slipping away to their homes or to various hostelries. There were odd flurries of snow and it was certainly no weather in which to be standing around outside. The travellers were able therefore to slip unseen into the close beside the shop, which led steeply down to the shore of the Nor' Loch.

Lizzie said good-bye to her aunt and uncle. 'Will you be all right Uncle David? We're sorry we've caused you so much trouble!'

'Och! Away with you!' replied the merchant. 'They'll forget in a day or two when something more exciting turns up.'

'What will happen to Thomas?' asked Lizzie suddenly remembering the reason they had gone back to Restalrig.

108

'Don't you worry about him,' reassured Uncle David. 'He's the sort that goes with the wind. He'll be easily persuaded I reckon to become a minister in the new Universal Kirk as so many of his fellow priests have done after a spell in the Castle dungeon. Then he'll be assigned to a parish. Who knows? Perhaps even Crail!'

Lizzie was relieved. They embraced briefly and then the travellers dissolved into the darkness down the close.

Gradually their eyes became accustomed to the dark and Lizzie drank in the sights eagerly, her eyes widening in astonishment with each new discovery. Their route was not a choice one, this being a general dumping ground for the rubbish of Edinburgh and rats squeaked beneath their feet, scuttling among the rotting debris.

They reached the Loch and squelched their way through slushy snow and ice along the boggy edge for what seemed a very long time. Lizzie could scarcely breathe at times for the stench in the air and longed suddenly for the clear salty fresh sea winds of her native Crail. They continued in silence until they felt themselves on drier, firmer ground when they were aware of a low whistle and a voice calling softly, 'Lizzie!'

Lizzie turned as she recognised the voice of Neil, one of her uncle's apprentices, and out of the shadow of a large rock saw him approach with a horse.

'The Master said to give this to you, Lizzie,' he whispered.

'Thank you. Thank you, Neil. And many thanks for everything! One day we shall return again I hope.'

'I hope so too,' replied Neil. 'We shall miss you.'

Walter mounted the horse and lifted Lizzie up in front of him. 'Thank you, Neil. Farewell.'

They set off with Neil's 'God speed!' still ringing in their ears.

Imprisoned

Ignoring their dazed cries for mercy and help, the ruffian band began to frog-march Davie and Father Thomas roughly away from Restalrig back in the direction of Edinburgh.

The way was dark and cold as they left the flames and heat of what was now an inferno behind them. They both tripped and stumbled as they were pushed mercilessly along, prodded from time to time by the butt of a wooden club. They could barely make out their captors in the darkness but it was clear from their conversation that there was one ring-leader whom they called the 'Master'. He it was who had been all for killing Davie and Father Thomas there and then at the Chapel. It had been the hunchback who had persuaded him otherwise and who now kept up a running commentary on all the various grotesque punishments they could dole out to their prisoners.

'Be sure there'll be no mercy for the likes of you!' he said in a low whine.

Davie hardly heard. He was quite numb at the thought of having lost Lizzie forever to a fate worse than death.

'It's all my fault,' he said miserably to himself. 'If only we hadn't gone back to try and save them!' At the thought of Thomas he was brought back to reality. Thomas was stumbling along beside him in a state of shock. Ever one to avoid argument and conflict he suddenly realised that all his fears of a tortuous death which he had dreaded ever since the Reformation had begun were now coming all too true. How he wished now that he had been killed outright like poor Father William. How he wished now that he had never come near the God-forsaken Chapel in the first place.

After what seemed an age they approached the city gates of Edinburgh at the Nether Bow. The 'Master' knocked three times on the guardhouse door with his heavy cudgel. It was obviously a signal to someone he knew inside for a guard soon appeared and with a rattling of keys let the little party through.

Up the main street the prisoners were led towards the Tol-booth. Their armed minders were in jovial mood at their success in capturing the prisoners and made plenty of shouting and mocking jests at the prisoners' expense. Though the streets were dark and deserted save for rats scurrying in the gutter Davie could sense that people hearing the noise of the rabble were watching from the several storeys of the high buildings that towered about them on either side. He was shivering with fear and desolate with worry. He knew that his uncle David was not far away, but there was no way of letting him know of his plight.

Eventually they came to the Tolbooth building. As they went in through a heavy door they were pushed into a cold damp room. At a table in the room on which was a lighted candle sat a young evil looking man who seemed to be in charge.

'Well, well!' he said. 'What have we here?' as the two prisoners were thrust roughly towards him.

'Two Papists from the Kirk at Restalrig, Captain' replied the 'Master', 'trying to thwart the order of the General Assembly to rase the building to the ground.'

At this point the hunchback stepped forward, rubbing his hands together gleefully.

'Begging your pardon Sir,' he said bowing towards the Captain at the table, 'but we thought we might make a public example of them. A flogging perhaps or even a burning?' He cackled evilly and his breath hung in a cloud around his mouth in the chilly air.

The dark haired man at the table looked thoughtfully at the gathering of ruffians and at the two prisoners who were trembling both with fear and the cold. It was late and he was wanting to go home to his warm bed. He was fed up with the Reformers starting up trouble again just when things seemed to be settling down nicely. Besides it was never the true believers at the thick of any fighting or unrest, but a small band of thugs and vagabonds who were only out to make trouble such as the motley band in front of him now.

'All right,' he commanded wearily, 'put them in there for the night. I'm away home.' He pointed to a room at the side. The heavy door with a metal grille in it was ajar and Davie and Thomas looked with some trepidation to the darkness beyond. Suddenly their captors pushed them towards it and the door was slammed behind them, a heavy key turning in the metal lock.

The room was pitch black and very cold and damp. Both the floor and walls were slimy and there didn't seem to be any window. Once their eyes got used to the darkness they could see the square grille in the door where the candle light shone through from the room they had just left.

'Oh dear! oh dear!' said Thomas clutching on to Davie's arm. 'What's to become of us? What will they do to us?'

'Wheesht man!' snapped Davie, tired and worried now. 'I'm sure I don't know what they'll do but babbling on about it won't help.'

Thomas fell silent. Davie suddenly felt sorry for him. Never a brave man by his own admission, it was to accompany them that Father Thomas had left the safe confines of the Nunnery at Haddington.

'Look, I'm sorry Father Thomas,' said Davie squeezing his shoulder in the pitch black. 'I'm sorry it had to come to this and

112

I'm sorry that Father William is dead, but most of all I'm sorry about Lizzie. It's all too terrible for words.' The strain of the day suddenly caught up with him and he broke down and sobbed into Thomas's arms.

After a while he felt better and the two peered in silence at the grille listening to the men outside. There was a lot of laughing and joking as they shared a jug of wine with each other.

Suddenly they heard a loud knocking at the outer door. It was opened and the noise among the company became instantly subdued.

'I wonder what's going on?' said Thomas to Davie as they tried to see what was happening. They could not believe their eyes or ears. Emerging into the candle light from the darkness of the doorway was David Cunningham.

'Uncle David! Uncle David!' shouted Davie for all he was worth. Mister Cunningham came rushing over looking extremely worried.

'Oh Davie, Davie! What have you got yourself into? Who's this in here with you?' and he peered into the blackness of their prison.

'It's Father Thomas,' explained Davie. 'Remember I told you he came with us from Haddington. He was at Restalrig when we went to rescue him. The other priest's dead.'

'Well,' replied his uncle, 'don't worry too much. I'll see what I can do for you, if only to get you moved perhaps to the Castle dungeons away from this rabble of ne'er-do-goods.' He pointed his thumb behind him. 'Don't worry anyway and keep your spirits up. All is not yet lost.'

He turned back to the company who had resumed their drinking.

'Now then,' he said, 'you can't keep a young lad and an innocent priest here. They haven't done anything to deserve this!'

Davie watching saw the hunchback sidle up to his uncle. 'Oh no? Just you wait and see the fun we have in store for them!'

The man they called the 'Master' took command of the situation.

'Just who do you think you are, sir?' he snarled, 'barging in here and interfering with the Queen's justice.'

'Queen's justice, my foot!' exclaimed David Cunningham forcefully. 'I'll have you know I am one of the Merchants of this city. I'll show you what the Queen's justice is! I shall get an order to remove these prisoners to the Castle. Mark my words! And you'll be sorry yet that you ever laid eyes on them!' So saying and with one last look towards the grille where Davie and Thomas were peering out hanging on his every word, he swept out.

The nasty hunchback came over to grille as the merchant left and spat at them.

'Bah!' he said, 'scum that you are. You'll pay the proper punishment yet and your Merchant friend may be lucky if he doesn't join you. It's not the done thing nowadays for the Merchants to support those of the Old Faith.' He gave them a triumphant leer confident that things would still go as he wished.

Davie and Thomas huddled dejectedly together in their prison cell and slept as well as they could. Unable to tell night from day it seemed an age to them before they heard another loud knock at the Tolbooth door.

'Open up in the name of the law!'

Davie and Thomas shivering in their cell watched bemused as half a dozen of the Castle Guards strode in, swords at the ready. Their spokesman waved a piece of paper beneath the nose of the man seated at the table.

'Orders from the Castle for the removal of the prisoners,' he said.

'Never!' said thè Captain jumping up and thumping a wine jug down emphatically on the table in front of him. 'You can't do this!'

The Guard grinned, 'Orders are orders, you know that sir! Now are you going to open up or do I have to use force?'

The man, realising that the soldier meant what he said, nodded stiffly to one of his men who limped slowly across with a bunch of keys and unlocked the door of the room where Davie and Thomas were held.

Davie did not know whether this change of events was good news for them or not. Would the Castle Guards be more merciful? Or would they leave them to rot in some deep dungeon for the rest of their lives?

They were pushed quickly out of the Tolbooth into the thick of a crowd which had gathered as news of the prisoners had spread. They were all intrigued to find out what the Castle soldiers were doing at the Tolbooth at this time of night. When it was realised that the prisoners were being moved the crowd fell to shouting and jeering.

The pair were marched briskly up the road with the mob roaring abuse behind them. Davie looked all around him drinking in the sights. If they were going to the Castle dungeons this might be the last he ever saw of the outside world.

They had not gone far when the Guards suddenly stopped and turned abruptly down a close to their right.

'Quick, in here!' ordered their leader.

To their surprise Davie and Thomas saw two men waiting down the alleyway with three horses.

'You laddie,' commanded the Guard briefly, pointing at Davie, 'on that horse. The priest comes with us.'

'No!' shouted Davie. 'We're staying together!' The Guard said not a word but drew his sword meaningfully and Davie mounted the horse immediately!

'Good bye Davie!' said Thomas bravely. 'Perhaps we'll meet in the next world.' The guards pulled him roughly by the arm out of the close again and the last Davie saw of him was marching up the street towards the Castle. They faded into the darkness but the sound of their boots and the clanking of their swords could be heard steadily receding into the distance.

One of the horsemen took hold of Davie's horse and led him the other way down the close they were in. The other man brought up the rear looking behind him every few seconds.

The smell was terrible and Davie realised they must be nearing

115

the Nor' Loch where all the rubbish lay. They eased their horses gently down the steep pathway and in no time at all they were splashing rapidly along the edge of the loch.

When they came to firmer ground, one of the men shouted, 'Now lad, gallop for your life! This way! After me!'

Davie's horse needed no bidding. As the other two took off it automatically followed after. Tired and exhausted though he was, Davie felt exhilarated to be out in the open again after the dank Tolbooth. Wherever they were taking him and whatever they planned to do with him, he no longer cared.

The wind whistled through his hair as he sped along.

Adventure at Sea

Walter and Lizzie galloped hard through the night. Snow blew softly into their faces as they rode, but the way to Leith was wide and even, so they made good progress and were soon down at the harbour.

The *Golden Lily* was still anchored at the quayside with her golden figurehead glinting in the moonlight.

Captain Scott came down the gang-plank to meet them when he saw them arrive.

'So you've decided to sail with me after all,' he teased Lizzie. She laughed and introduced Walter and told him how she was able to see again.

'So the Well is miraculous indeed,' said the Captain thoughtfully looking at her and laughing at her obvious delight in being able to see. 'Pity you couldn't have told the General Assembly that - but it would probably be unwise. After all it was the falling down the stairs that did it or so they'd say.'

'It was a miracle,' said Lizzie quietly and that seemed to be the last word on the matter. Even Walter only smiled and said nothing.

'Come now,' said Captain Scott urgently. 'The wind is rising and my sailors are at the ready. We are just waiting to see if Davie will arrive. I don't like to sail at night but the Master is concerned that the mob might follow Davie if they discover that he has escaped. Listen! I think that may be him now.'

There was the sound of galloping hooves on the cobbles as three horses came hurriedly on to the quay. One of the riders jumped down. It was Davie!

Looking unharmed he hugged Lizzie happily with tears in his eyes when she told him she could really see but he was taken aback to see Walter standing with her. Captain Scott herded them briskly on to his ship before Lizzie could explain.

'We have to sail at once,' he said as he hurried up the gang-plank after them, glancing anxiously over his shoulder as he heard more shouting in the distance. 'I fear they may have already discovered Davie's escape.'

They were lucky. The wind was favourable for them and the sails were quickly hoisted by the Captain's men so that they could glide off into the darkness.

Davie, Lizzie, and Walter once aboard found some shelter from the bitter winter wind inside the hold. They huddled together in the blankets that Mistress Cunningham had so kindly provided and Lizzie explained to Davie all that had happened since she had fallen down the stairs at St Triduana's Chapel and how she had been looked after by Walter. How Walter had been the ominous leper and how he had eventually rescued her from Restalrig.

'Well, well,' said Davie in wonderment as she told of the recovery of her sight and how Walter disguised as a leper had rescued her from the clutches of the unruly mob.

'And were you the leper who was dogging our footsteps all the way from Gullane? I should have known!'

'Aye, it was me all right. And a good job too as it turned out.' Walter shuddered at the thought of what might have happened to Lizzie and indeed Davie if he had not been there.

He held out a hand to Davie, 'Davie, laddie, there are some things that have to be said. I've not been a good father to you I

118

know that but this past wee while I've learnt a thing or two and
... well ...' He paused, fumbling for words, 'well, I'd like to
make up for it if you can find it in you to forgive me and let the
two of us be friends.'

Davie, surprised, took his hand and shook it. Things were
happening so fast that he was having difficulty taking it all in.
Something had happened to Walter. He was not the same man
that they had fled from at all. There was more than one miracle
in the air!

'Aye, certainly Walter, let's be friends. I know I've no' been
the kind of son you would have hoped for either but what made
you change your mind about catching us? Don't tell me that you
have returned to the Old Faith?'

Walter shook his head. 'Mercy, no, Davie. I'm still as staunch
a supporter of the Reforms as I ever was but I've had some
good long talks with yon John Knox and he's made me see
that a certain measure of tolerance is necessary otherwise we
are no better than the Catholics we condemn.' He shrugged
his shoulders and laughed. 'Perhaps what caused my change
of heart towards you most of all was the smoked fish you
left out for me that very first day when you thought I was
a leper. I don't think I've ever been in sorer need of food
than then.'

Davie smiled. 'If it hadn't been for Gilbert the Friar we were
travelling with offering to put out his last crust I don't think I
would have given you a crumb.'

Lizzie looked happily from one to the other.

'Never mind,' she said, 'at least it's all over now and we're all
together again.'

Davie then told the other two how he had suddenly been set
free by the Castle Guards and hustled out of Edinburgh by two
men he had never seen before who had bade him mount a horse
and follow them.

'I think that you have your Uncle David to thank for that and
at great risk to his own standing in the city,' said Walter.

Davie nodded. 'I thought as much though I have to admit at

the time I thought that they were leading me out to hang me there and then, so you can imagine the relief when I saw the *Golden Lily* and yourselves.'

Presently Captain Scott came down to see them.

'I'm afraid that the journey is going to take a bit longer since the weather is worsening. I had hoped to reach Crail by dawn to avoid any possibility of pirates, but it is going to be midday at least before we get near it.'

Davie and Lizzie slept fitfully through the night tucked in beside their step-father as the boat rolled and heaved in the water but with the coming of the dawn the wind lessened and they were able to look out over the grey seas. A light covering of snow and frost covered the land but there was no mistaking where they were.

Davie shouted excitedly. 'Come and look Lizzie! It's the Bay of Elie and Earlsferry!'

Lizzie looked with wonder as they passed all the places that she had only heard of and her excitement mounted at the thought of seeing her mother. Soon they were passing Pittenweem. Davie pointed out the Priory to her.

'Here we are safe home again, Lizzie. It'll no' be much longer now!'

But they had not reckoned on fate. Shortly after Pittenweem there was an order from the Captain to get below. There was a pirate ship approaching and there could be fighting.

'Oh no,' thought Davie. 'Surely we haven't come through everything only to be drowned within sight of home.'

They crouched in their hiding place as they heard the orders flying above.

'Heave about, *Golden Lily* ! Prepare to deliver your cargo!' a voice called over the water.

'Never!' they could hear Captain Scott shouting back. 'Never as long as I live.'

'Men! Prepare to board!' shouted the other voice. 'Bring her alongside!'

There was the sound of feet thudding on the deck and blood-curdling yells as sword and stave clashed against each other. Walter told Lizzie and Davie to stay in the hold while he went up on deck to give help. For a while the two huddled together fearfully listening to the sound of fighting. Never had either of them heard such a dreadful noise as the sound of the moaning wounded men. When Davie could stand the noise no longer he got up.

'I'm going up to help too, Lizzie! I can't just sit around here listening to that. You stay here!'

'Oh! Davie! Take care!' was all Lizzie had time to say before her brother disappeared from view.

As he climbed out of the hold Davie grabbed one of the large hooks they used to close the hatches. It had been warm and muggy down there and as he climbed the ladder the air grew noticeably cooler. In the grey winter light he hardly had time to take in the scene on deck before someone sprang on him from behind. He staggered under the impact but flailed out with the hook behind him and felt his assailant release his grip as the hook caught his leg. Davie turned immediately to face his attacker, a lanky looking lad not much older than himself, as the pirate lurched to recover his balance. In one hand he held a large dagger which glinted as he raised it high to come down again upon Davie. Davie braced himself for the blow but the boat heaved at that very moment and the pirate stepped back tripping over a body lying on the deck and toppled backwards. Davie watched him fall. By rights he ought to go in now and at least knock him out while he had the advantage but he could not bring himself to do it. Suddenly Walter was at his side.

'Well done, Davie! I'm proud of you.' he said quickly.

'But what do we do with him now, Walter?' asked Davie worriedly as the man began to pick himself up again. 'Shall we tie him up?'

Walter winked at him and his face broke into a smile.

'Haven't time for that, laddie. No! Simpler than that . . .' and he strode forward, picked up the protesting man by the belt of his breeks and in one easy throw tossed him overboard. The man let out a long drawn out wail. Then there was a splash and silence as he hit the water. Davie was gaping open-mouthed in astonishment at his step-father, who saw him and laughed.

'Och I've a few tricks you don't know about, Davie!' he joked. 'Come on! Back to battle! Stick by me!'

They made their way slowly towards the bow of the ship fighting as they went. They worked together, Davie drawing each pirate's attention by waving his hook, allowing Walter to come in from the side or the back. Walter's height meant that he was able to lift the men by the scruff of the neck. Most of them went over the side like the first accompanied by a shout of victory from Walter and Davie saw them scrambling hurriedly on to their own ship again. No-one would last long in these icy waters.

Meanwhile he was aware of a commotion up at the front of the ship and looking up in horror saw Captain Scott set in armed combat with none other than Alan's friend Captain Lumsden and the pirate Captain was clearly getting the better of the tussle. Davie gasped and rushed towards them to try and rescue Captain Scott but someone leapt on him from behind. He struggled for breath as the pirate on his back throttled him and struck out wildly with his hook to no avail. Where was Walter? he thought, choking desperately.

'Davie!' Walter's voice cried out in alarm and he could feel the person who was strangling him relax his hold as he was hauled off by a strong arm. He turned round stiffly to see Walter on the point of throwing his attacker into the water and was shocked to see that it was none other than Alan Maynard!

'Alan!' he cried in astonishment.

Realising that the two knew each other Walter released his grip momentarily. There was not time to explain to Walter.

'Oh, Alan!' cried Davie. 'Please help! Captain Lumsden is going to kill the Captain!'

Rooted weakly to the spot, it seemed like an age to Davie as he watched Alan with Walter at his heels make his way swiftly to the prow of the ship where Captain Lumsden now had Captain Scott pinned to the gunwale by the point of his sword.

'Stop! Stop!' shouted Alan in alarm. 'Stop, Captain Lumsden!'

Lumsden was taken aback for a split second and in that moment Walter stepped in. He knocked the man to the side as if he were a feather and Captain Scott sprang to his feet immediately as Lumsden fell to the deck. Scott retrieving his sword raised it over him.

'I should kill you, you scoundrel,' he said, the dashing captain once more, now that he had the other at his mercy. 'What do you mean by attacking my ship?'

'I — I truly thought you were an English ship, Captain. Spare my life!' replied the pirate pleading pathetically now that he realised that he had lost the day.

'Aye,' shouted Davie breathlessly, running up. 'Please spare him! He's a friend of a friend of mine.'

'This cut-throat pirate! A friend of yours, young Davie? I might have known! I don't think anything about you would surprise me now! All right Captain get up! I spare your life this once because of the lad Davie here but I am going to commandeer your ship and crew.' Captain Lumsden sat up shocked by the turnabout in his fortune and looked along the ship to see Lizzie walking towards him across the deck.

'That lassie again!' he said in surprise. 'I might have known! I knew she was bad luck the minute I set eyes on her!'

Captain Scott interrupted. 'On the contrary, my man, it is instead your lucky day. I have spared your life.'

He prodded the pirate with the point of his sword.

'Into that boat there Captain and start rowing before I change my mind.' He indicated a small rowing boat which was tied up at the side of his ship and Captain Lumsden climbed in. He started rowing in the direction of Cellardyke which was in fact not too far off. Captain Scott watched him set off then turned back to the group on his deck.

124

'Now then, this is your friend is it, Davie?' He patted Alan on the shoulder and the latter smiled sheepishly. 'Well, lad,' he continued, 'you saved my life at the risk of your own and certainly to the loss of your own livelihood. How can I repay you?'

Alan shuffled his feet. 'Don't you worry about me Captain. I'll aye make out. I saved your life for the sake of Davie here, nothing more.'

Walter stepped forward. 'I'd like to make a suggestion in everybody's interests if I may.'

'Carry on,' said Captain Scott.

'Well I'd like to make Alan the offer of a job with me on the fishing boat. I've aye looked forward to the day when I'd have my son to help me. I'm no' getting any younger now and Davie's no' interested in anything but his books and his learning. What say you Alan to becoming a second son in the Fisher household?'

Alan astounded looked closely at the dark fisherman's face but the offer seemed genuine. Then he looked at Davie. Surely this was not the same Walter Fisher who been chasing his stepchildren so furiously only a month or so back? Davie laughed at his surprise and nodded as if to second the suggestion. Lizzie ran forward.

'Aye, Alan,' she cried gleefully, 'go on! Come and live with us!'

Alan shook his head slowly. 'Well,' he said, 'If the lovely Lizzie says aye, who am I to refuse?' They all laughed and Lizzie blushed to the roots.

'Then that's settled,' said Walter and the Captain in chorus and Alan and Walter shook hands on it.

Captain Scott then sent some of his sailors who had not been injured in the fighting across to the pirate ship to take it in tow and the *Golden Lily* continued on her way.

Meanwhile, Alan, delighted at the way that fate had given him a home and family once more, listened excitedly to their adventures and the miracle that had happened to Lizzie.

They were at Crail before they knew it and a little boat was lowered to row the party ashore. They thanked the Captain and climbed into the small boat.

By this time a crowd had gathered on the harbour wall, curious to see who should be landing from such a large and prosperous looking ship. As the little craft came in closer to shore, a woman finally recognised Davie and ran off shrieking to find Jeannie.

'Jeannie! Jeannie! It's Davie and Lizzie!' she shouted. 'Oh my! Oh my!' The woman disappeared into a house and by the time the little boat had entered the harbour she had reappeared with Jeannie Cunningham.

Lizzie watched fascinated at all the sights around her. This was the moment she had been waiting for and now that it was here she hoped that she would not be disappointed.

They climbed up on to the harbour wall from the boat and embraced their mother.

'I can see, Mother! I can see!' shouted Lizzie and to her astonishment her mother burst into tears.

'Oh my bairns, oh my bairns,' was all she could say. Then she noticed Walter climbing out of the boat too. 'Walter!' she exclaimed not sure what to say to him. It was a good three months since he had run out of the house after the children.

'I've brought them back safely to you,' he said simply. It was explanation enough.

'Thank you,' she whispered. 'Thank you for looking after them.' He smiled and put an arm round her shoulders, tears in his own eyes.

'Come on Jeannie. We've a lot to talk about.'

A cannon fired in salute and they all turned to see the *Golden Lily*, with the pirate ship still in tow, glide off towards Holland.

Then Davie and Lizzie led their mother through the excited crowd slowly up the cobbled harbour slope to their house. Walter and Alan followed at a short distance.

'This calls for a celebration,' said Jeannie wiping the tears from her eyes as they reached the house. She made straight for the chimney lum from which she drew in triumph five fish. 'Now let me cook these and you shall tell me all about everything — especially the miracle,' she smiled, giving Lizzie a squeeze.

126

'Not quite yet, Mother,' interrupted Davie. 'Walter can give you all the details and introduce you to Alan for I have a promise to keep,' and he grinned at Lizzie. Jeannie smiled to see the twinkle in her daughter's eyes, still hardly daring to believe that the impossible had happened.

'And what is that promise?' she asked.

'I promised Lizzie that as soon as we got home I would take her to see the view from the cliff-top where we always used to sit.'

'All right,' she smiled, 'but don't be long!' And the sound of their happy voices disappearing into the distance was like music to her ears.

THE END